KT-501-641

Defy
the
Stars

Also by Sophie McKenzie

SPLIT SECOND

FALLING FAST
BURNING BRIGHT
CASTING SHADOWS

GIRL, MISSING
SISTER, MISSING
MISSING ME

BLOOD TIES
BLOOD RANSOM

SIX STEPS TO A GIRL
THREE'S A CROWD
THE ONE AND ONLY

THE MEDUSA PROJECT 1: *THE SET-UP*
THE MEDUSA PROJECT 2: *THE HOSTAGE*
THE MEDUSA PROJECT WORLD BOOK DAY SPECIAL:
THE THIEF
THE MEDUSA PROJECT 3: *THE RESCUE*
THE MEDUSA PROJECT 4: *HUNTED*
THE MEDUSA PROJECT 5: *DOUBLE-CROSS*
THE MEDUSA PROJECT 6: *HIT SQUAD*

Defy the Stars
the

SOPHIE McKENZIE

SIMON AND SCHUSTER

Acknowledgements: with thanks to Moira Young, Gaby Halberstam, Julie Mackenzie, Melanie Edge and Lou Kuenzler.

First published in Great Britain in 2014 by Simon and Schuster UK Ltd,
a CBS company

Copyright © 2014 Rosefire Ltd

Lyrics from 'The Power of Love' by Frankie Goes to Hollywood appear by
kind permission of Perfect Songs. © 1984. All rights reserved.

This book is copyright under the Berne Convention.
No reproduction without permission.
All rights reserved.

The right of Sophie McKenzie to be identified as the author of
this work has been asserted by her in accordance with sections
77 and 78 of the Copyright, Designs and Patents Act, 1988.

Simon & Schuster UK Ltd
1st Floor, 222 Gray's Inn Road, London, WC1X 8HB

This book is a work of fiction. Names, characters, places and incidents are
either the product of the author's imagination or are used fictitiously. Any
resemblance to actual people living or dead, events or locales is entirely
coincidental.

A CIP catalogue record for this book is available from the British Library.

PB ISBN: 978-0-85707-105-7
EBOOK ISBN 978-0-85707-106-4

1 3 5 7 9 10 8 6 4 2

Printed and bound by CPI Group (UK) Ltd, Croydon, CR0 4YY

www.simonandschuster.co.uk
www.simonandschuster.com.au

In memory of Nancy, Celia and Monica
and the stories they told.

Is it even so? then I defy you, stars!
Romeo and Juliet (Act 5, Scene 1)

1

Dad woke me in the middle of the night.

I opened my eyes to find his weather-beaten face looming anxiously over mine. The room was dark, though a faint light crept in through the open window.

'River?'

I blinked, bleary-eyed, at him. 'What time is it? What's wrong?'

'Just gone four,' he said. 'I need your help.'

I sat up, suddenly afraid. 'What's the matter? Is it Gemma?'

Dad's girlfriend Gemma was pregnant, though her baby wasn't due for another six weeks.

'No, Gemma's fine. I just don't want to wake her. It's that last Jacob sheep. She's been in labour for the past hour. The generator's gone down and I need you to bring out some lamps. I've got to go straight back. Okay?'

1

'Sure. I'll be right there.'

Dad vanished. I sat in bed for a second, psyching myself up for the dash out from under the covers to get my clothes. It was always cold in the commune at night, even when the daytimes were sunny.

I took a deep breath and threw back the covers. The air nipped at my arms and feet as I pulled on sweatpants over my pyjamas, plus two pairs of socks, a fleece and a jumper. Downstairs I slipped on my boots and one of Dad's woolly hats which was lying on the kitchen table. Not exactly a glamorous look, I thought, as I fetched the three hurricane lamps from their cupboard by the back door.

I tried to make an effort at sixth form college, remembering to put on earrings and a bit of make-up before I headed off each day. I did that to show people – especially Dad – that I was fully over my relationship with Flynn. It had ended last year when Flynn found out about a meaningless, two-second kiss I'd had ages before with his best friend, James.

I had only seen Flynn once since then – a few weeks later – when he'd sought me out for a few minutes to apologise for the way he'd vanished so angrily. Up until that point I'd done nothing but hate myself, but afterwards I started to move on.

That was seventeen weeks, two days and three-and-a-half hours ago.

I filled the three hurricane lanterns with paraffin, lit them and headed out to the barn. The pre-dawn air was damp and cold, the grass at my feet glistening with dew. The barn was in virtual darkness when I arrived, just Dad's torch sending flickering shadows across the walls. The sheep was on her side, her belly twitching as the lamb inside moved. Dad was stroking her flank, murmuring softly.

'Come on, girl, you can do it.' He looked up as I walked in. 'I think she's close, Riv. The miracle of birth in our own barn, eh?'

I rolled my eyes. Dad had always been a bit of a romantic hippy about stuff like birth and the cycle of life. He was in his element on the commune. Over the past year I had grown to like it too, though I definitely didn't see myself living here forever. I didn't have strong feelings about where I would go or what I would do. But then, I didn't feel strongly about anything. Since Flynn had gone, nothing seemed to touch me in quite the same way any more.

'Put the lamps over there,' Dad said.

I placed the lanterns carefully, then squatted down next to him. The minutes ticked away. The sky outside was shot through with pink now, but still no lamb, although the sheep was clearly getting more and more uncomfortable.

3

'I think we're going to have to give her a bit of a hand,' Dad said.

I held the sheep steady while Dad felt for the lamb. He talked the whole time. When he wasn't soothing the sheep, he was exclaiming about how amazing it was to witness birth like this. We kept about fifteen sheep on the commune and so far this season only two others had needed help delivering their lambs.

There were tears in Dad's eyes as he pulled the latest newborn free by her legs. 'Wow,' he said. 'It never stops being miraculous, does it?'

I bent down to free some of the gloop around the tiny lamb's mouth, then rubbed it vigorously with a handful of hay.

'Never stops being messy,' I said with a grunt.

Dad sighed. 'You should get up to the house, River. I can finish here.'

I stared down at the baby. The first time I'd seen a newborn I'd been shocked by how ugly it was – nothing like the frisky white lambs you see bouncing around in fields. I knew that it *was* amazing to witness a birth, so why couldn't I *feel* that it was amazing? All I had felt for months, it seemed, was a dull ache in my chest. I wasn't unhappy any longer – I'd accepted Flynn wasn't coming back – I just couldn't seem to get really excited about anything

4

either. Still, maybe that was what most people's lives were like, maybe this was normal.

'Isn't there a second lamb?' I asked.

Dad shook his head. 'Nah, just the one this time. It's her first.' He sighed. 'Like it will be for Gemma soon.'

I sat back and yawned. 'Well I hope you don't have to pull my little brother or sister out by the legs.'

'*River!*' Dad grinned.

We sat, watching, as the sheep nuzzled at the baby and the little lamb started moving. It was properly light outside now. I could see the sun rising in the blue sky. It was going to be another beautiful day.

I stood up and stretched.

'Go on, go back to bed,' Dad said. 'You've got sixth form in the morning. Those exams coming up.'

I snorted. 'Dad, it *is* morning.'

Dad checked his watch. '*Goodness*, it's nearly half past six.' He glanced at me, a guilty shadow flitting across his face. 'I'm sorry, River, I—'

'It's fine, Dad,' I said. 'I've got three private study periods today. I can take it easy.'

'Good.' Dad gave me a hug. He was yawning himself now.

'Is everything okay?' It was Leo. He was standing in the barn doorway, a slight figure casting a long thin shadow over the hay.

'Yup,' Dad said proudly. 'One lamb, safely delivered. Come see.'

The three of us stood looking down at the lamb which was now struggling to its feet. Leo was already dressed in his clothes for college – black trousers and a long-sleeved top under a cotton jacket. He'd obviously just showered as his fine blond hair was still wet.

'Wow, that's brilliant,' Leo said.

Dad beamed at him.

'Er, I'm making toast in the kitchen,' Leo went on.

'Excellent.' Dad rubbed his hands together. 'River, you go on ahead. I just want to make sure everything's okay here.'

Leo and I walked up to the main commune building in a companionable silence. Leo was, at this stage, pretty much my best friend and in the same year as me at the local sixth form college.

'Dad's talking about moving out of the commune,' Leo said, jolting me out of my reverie.

'What?' I turned to him, shocked. 'Why?'

'He and Ros want to move in together,' Leo explained. 'They're talking about leaving the commune, going to another part of the country to live.'

'Really?' I was surprised. Ros, another member of the commune, had got together with Leo's dad last

6

year. They'd been sickeningly into each other ever since, but Ros had always been adamant she would never live 'in patriarchal monogamy' with a man after her previous series of disastrous relationships. 'How d'you feel about that?' I asked.

Leo shrugged. I was guessing it was hard for him to see his dad with someone else. His mum died just a couple of years ago and I knew Leo missed her a lot. I followed Leo into the commune kitchen. It was empty, though the smell of toast wafted deliciously towards us. I headed for the sink and filled the kettle with water.

'How I feel about it depends on you,' Leo said.

I stopped, my hand on the kettle. Leo and I had grown close after Flynn and I split up. Leo made it clear around that time that he'd like us to be even closer, but he'd accepted our friendship and I thought he understood that going out together just wasn't an option. The whole issue hadn't been mentioned for months, in fact, and I was seriously hoping Leo had got over me.

'Does it?' I said, trying to keep my voice light. 'Why's that?'

'You know why,' Leo mumbled. 'I need to know if there's any point me staying for . . . for *us*.'

I pressed the on switch on the kettle. Then took a deep breath.

'We're friends, Leo, and I really value that. But there isn't an "*us*". Not like that.'

'What about in the future?'

I frowned. This was agony, really awkward. I knew that I should tell Leo I would never go out with him but it seemed too cruel to be so direct.

'I don't know, Leo,' I said. 'I'm sorry.'

Leo nodded, then he left the room. I buttered my toast and sat at the table. Why did life have to be so complicated?

After a while the rest of the commune appeared, each of them in turn trooping out to the barn to check on the new arrival. Gemma was the last to arrive. She looked tired, with dark rings under her eyes. Her pregnant belly stuck out in front of her. It looked huge but then, as Leo had privately pointed out, that was partly because Gemma herself was so tiny.

'There's some post for you, River. I just saw it on the mat.' She grimaced. 'Sorry I didn't pick it up but bending down at the moment is a nightmare.'

I got up and headed out to the hall. I needed to go upstairs and get showered and dressed, ready for college. Wondering whether I had time to wash my hair, I picked up the large, flat envelope and opened it absently.

It contained an invitation from Flynn's sister, Siobhan:

Siobhan Daniella Mary Flynn

and

Gary Goode

request the honour of your presence at their

marriage

on Saturday 17 May at 3pm

at the Church of Our Lady, Harrow

followed by a party at Lyttenham House.

My heart thumped as a single question threaded through my head: would Flynn be there? I turned over the card. Siobhan had scrawled a note on the back:

Dear River, hope v much u will be able to make it. U were the first person after Mum I ever told about Gary and it would mean a lot if u came. Thought u wd want to know Flynn will be there too. (Mum is over moon!) Just so u also know, he will be bringing a friend. U can bring someone too if u like. Really hope u can make it. Lotsa love S xxxxx

The hallway spun around me. I put my hand against the wall to steady myself. So Flynn *would* be there. And not alone either. Bringing 'a friend' meant a girlfriend. Didn't it? Jealousy flickered at the edges of my mind.

9

I pushed the dark feelings away. I was *so* over Flynn. I only thought about him now maybe once or twice a day. My decision shouldn't be based on our old relationship.

The question was simple: did I want to go?

The wedding was in three weeks and would mean taking the day off from my new Saturday waitressing job. Still, I'd like to go for Siobhan. And it would be nice to see Flynn's mum and little sister Caitlin again as well. But how would it feel to see *him*?

I tucked the invitation back in its envelope and headed upstairs for my shower. I shouldn't go. There was no point raking up the past again.

On the other hand, I couldn't deny I was curious. And I'd already moved on so far, maybe seeing Flynn would be the final bit of closure that I needed to lay the whole relationship firmly to rest. I grabbed some clean clothes and headed into the bathroom.

I would have liked to call Emmi and ask her opinion but I hadn't spoken to my former best friend since she'd betrayed me to Flynn over the stupid kiss that had sent him storming out of my life last year.

Still, I had to talk to somebody. Leo was no good; he disliked Flynn. I settled on Grace. She had always been a good friend and fair-minded about Flynn. It was true that the kiss that had caused all the problems had been between me and Grace's boyfriend James, but Grace – unlike Flynn – had understood exactly how meaningless the whole thing had been.

I was seeing her later, after school. I'd make up my mind about Siobhan's wedding when I'd talked to her. It wasn't that big a deal. The point was that I was over Flynn. The rest was just the dust settling around the fact of us being apart. Seeing him again wouldn't – couldn't – make any difference to that.

2

Grace was in an anxious mood when I met her, worrying about the upcoming exams. She still went to the school I'd left last year when Flynn and I had moved to the commune and started at the local sixth form college. Sometimes I missed my old school but then, when I heard Grace talking about all the silly rules they still had even for older girls, I was glad I'd left and gone somewhere where you got treated in a more grown-up way.

I listened to Grace fret about some piece of work she'd just handed in for her Business Studies course, reassuring her that she had probably done better than she imagined.

'You know what you're like,' I said. 'It's never as bad as you think.'

Grace made a face. 'It's just I should have worked harder. I'm not like you and Emmi, do nothing for weeks then a bit of last-minute effort and an easy A.'

I snorted, trying to ignore this mention of Emmi. Grace often brought her up. I think she hoped Emmi and I might one day become friends again.

'Emmi's got a new boyfriend, you know,' Grace said timidly.

'There's a surprise.' I couldn't keep the bitterness out of my voice when I talked about her. It might all be water under the bridge, but it still hurt that Emmi had told Flynn about my nano-kiss.

There was an awkward silence, then James walked in.

'Hi, River.' He smiled across the room at me as Grace fluttered over to kiss him.

'I didn't know you were here,' she said, giving him a hug.

'Your mum let me in,' James went on.

He sat down and started chatting about which festival he and Grace should go to later in the summer. My heart sank. It was nice to see James of course, but I hadn't expected him to arrive this early and I hadn't had a chance to ask Grace what she thought about me seeing Flynn again yet. Still, James had once been Flynn's closest friend and, though they'd fallen out last year too, it would be interesting to know what he thought about Flynn and me meeting once more. James was solid and unemotional – I couldn't imagine he would think it was all that big a deal.

'Hey, guys . . .' I explained the situation.

As I spoke, Grace's eyes widened with concern.

'So what do you think?' I asked. 'I'd like to go and Flynn and I have been over for ages. It's fine, isn't it?'

James and Grace looked at each other, then back at me.

'Come on,' I said. 'According to his sister's note he's obviously got a girlfriend and everything – there's nothing between us any more.'

'Are you sure?' Grace asked with a frown. 'It's just, I know you're over him and everything, but it would still be hard to be friends, wouldn't it?'

'We're not talking about being friends.' I rolled my eyes. 'It's just saying "hello" at a wedding, for goodness sake. What do you think, James?'

James levelled his gaze at me. 'Honestly, River?' he said with a sigh. 'I like Flynn a lot, but I think you two being in the same room again is a *really* bad idea.'

'Why?' I said.

James shrugged. 'It just is.'

Surprised, I settled back against the wall and changed the subject back to summer festivals. Soon James and Grace were debating the various merits of the big name venues. I said very little, lost in my own thoughts. James and Grace were wrong to be so concerned about me seeing Flynn. And the fact

14

that I felt that so strongly made it easy, finally, to decide: I would go to the wedding. I would see Flynn. That would be that.

Having told Siobhan I was coming, I needed to get hold of two final things: a new dress and the best-looking date I could find.

Acquiring the dress turned out to be fairly straightforward. I hadn't bought anything new since the outfit I'd worn to our party last October, when Flynn and I had split up. Dad was only too delighted when I asked if I could do some additional chores at the commune in order to get some cash to pay for something new to wear. He even gave me a bit of extra money on top. I went shopping with Grace and found a pretty, dark red dress with a long, tight-fitting skirt that, I hoped, made my short legs look longer. Grace said it did, anyway. She was in a far better mood than when I'd seen her the other day, saying she had just decided she wanted to train as a primary school-teacher after leaving sixth form at the end of next year. However, her face fell when I confided that I was buying the dress specifically to look good at Siobhan's wedding.

'Oh, Riv,' she said, a deep frown creasing her forehead. 'I know you say you're over Flynn but . . .

15

you wouldn't go out with him again, would you? I mean . . . it would be *crazy* to go back.'

I reassured her that I was only going to the wedding to support Siobhan, and that I only wanted to look my best out of respect for her.

'Anyway,' I said with a grin. 'Everyone knows that weddings are a brilliant place to meet new people. Flynn won't be the only guy in the room; I've got to look good.'

This led to a lengthy conversation during which Grace tried to get me to consider practically every boy we knew as a potential boyfriend. I rejected them all as too boring, too weird or 'just not right', then went back to the commune to face another long talk with Dad. He told me that although he trusted me to know what was right for me, and was happy for me to go to Siobhan's wedding, he was still worried that if I wasn't careful, seeing Flynn might prompt me to 'slip back' into the misery of 'those early days without him'.

I couldn't really blame Dad for worrying. He had been in the front row, watching helplessly as I fell apart immediately after my break-up with Flynn, when I stayed in bed and didn't speak to anyone for a week.

I listened to his warning, then told him, with total honesty, that there was no chance of me going back

16

to the state I was in then. I tried to reassure Leo too, but with less success. He told me quietly he knew I still had feelings for Flynn, even if I denied them to myself. He also offered to come with me to the wedding. I said no, mostly for Leo's sake. The last time the two of them had seen each other, Flynn had punched Leo, leaving him with a huge bruise on his face for days. I didn't want to risk any repeat of that.

Instead I set my sights on a date with Michael Greene, a tall, buff guy in the year above me – Flynn's year – at college. He was so unlikely a choice as a proper boyfriend that he hadn't even featured on Grace's list. Still, he would be the perfect partner for a long day out when I needed someone attractive and easy-going on my arm. Michael wasn't the smartest student academically but he was one of the nicest boys I'd ever met. He wanted to work with animals and already spent a lot of his spare time volunteering with the RSPCA. He knew that Leo and I lived on a commune with hens and sheep and had already asked me many times about the animals and how we cared for them, so after considering how to approach him for a few days, I invited him round to check out the new baby lamb.

He was over the moon, really excited to see the lamb, overawed by the fact that I'd helped deliver it and full of questions for Dad, which Dad was only too delighted to answer. I explained carefully to Michael that I was looking for someone to come with me to the wedding . . . not as a date, but as a friend.

Michael frowned, confusion in his soft brown eyes. 'What about Leo?' he said, in his deep, slow voice.

I gulped. Clearly Michael, like most of our sixth form college, assumed that Leo and I were an item. I explained that it was Flynn's sister getting married and that Flynn himself would be present. Michael, who knew Flynn from the time he'd spent with us at college last year, understood straight away.

And so I was sorted. I'd cancelled my normal Saturday shift at the Rainbow Café, I'd got my dress and I had tall, hunky Michael Greene to stand beside me. Michael had even promised to wear a suit.

The closer the wedding got, the calmer I felt. After all, I hadn't seen Flynn for five months. We hadn't spoken or written to each other in all that time. This meeting was simply going to be the final sign-off. I would probably never see him again afterwards. It would give me the only thing I still needed, something that the counsellor I saw last year had even suggested I should try to find, the 'full stop' at the end of the relationship.

Of course I couldn't help but feel a bit nervous on

the morning of the wedding. Leo saw I was anxious and tried to talk to me, but I brushed aside his question, saying my nerves had nothing to do with seeing Flynn later, that I was just fretting about my exams starting at the end of the following week.

It was another sunny day – crisp and cooler than we'd been having recently. I washed and dried my hair carefully, taking far more trouble than usual. Well, it was a wedding. I put on a dab of make-up, even applying some of the dark red lipstick which I'd bought to go with my new dress. I was wearing high heels and one of Gemma's little black jackets over the dress.

I checked myself out in the full-length bathroom mirror once I was ready. Not too bad. At least the dress suited my curvy shape, the shape of the skirt plus the heels definitely made my legs look longer – and there was a flush in my cheeks that gave my skin a glow I knew it hadn't had for months.

Dad raised his eyebrows as I walked into the kitchen.

'Very sophisticated,' he said with a smile. 'I hope Michael knows how glamorous he needs to be to keep up with you.'

I rolled my eyes. Since Michael's visit a few weeks ago, Dad appeared to think we were now dating. I had decided not to correct this assumption. It would, surely, help Dad to face the idea of me seeing Flynn if he believed I was interested in another boy.

The doorbell rang. Leo shouted out to say he'd let Michael in. Leo, of course, knew exactly why I'd asked Michael to be my date.

The two of them appeared in the kitchen a few seconds later. They both stared at me.

'Bit of a change from sweatpants,' I said, feeling my face flush.

'You look amazing,' Michael said. He was, as he'd promised, dressed in a suit with a crisp white shirt and carefully waxed hair.

'Looking good yourself,' I grinned.

Leo cleared his throat. 'Nice dress, River,' he said. He was smiling, but I could see the unhappiness in his eyes. Was he upset because I was going to see Flynn? Or because he thought I might be seriously interested in Michael Greene? Either way, it wasn't the reaction of a person content just to be my friend.

My heart sank. 'Er, thanks,' I said.

'Time to go.' Dad stood up. He'd offered a while back to drive Michael and me to the wedding.

Leo disappeared upstairs. I watched him go, feeling concerned. A few minutes later, however, we were in the car and my thoughts turned to the wedding ahead. I took a few deep breaths, trying to calm the butterflies suddenly zooming around my stomach. It was just the prospect of meeting a bunch of strangers that was making me so nervous, I told myself. Nothing to do with seeing Flynn again. I remembered Siobhan's note about Flynn bringing a friend and felt relieved to have Michael at my side. I was sure it would be easy enough to be friendly with whoever Flynn was now going out with but the situation was definitely helped by my having my own date present.

Dad and Michael talked all the way. Then Dad dropped us outside the church where people were milling about. I couldn't spot anyone I knew, so Michael and I headed inside. The church was packed. Gary, Siobhan's fiancé, was up at the front but there was no sign of Flynn.

A lot of the people here were just a few years older than I was – and very dressed up in suits and dresses. Most of the girls were slim and pretty. I recognised a couple from the hair salon where Siobhan used to work. I smoothed the skirt of my dress down, hoping I didn't look too bad in comparison.

I could tell Michael felt a bit anxious too. He was fingering the collar of his shirt and there were beads of sweat on his forehead. For a moment, I wished I was here with Leo. At least he and I could have chatted about something to take our minds off the occasion. Michael and I didn't really have much in common. He was studying science and business studies at college whereas I was doing arts subjects. Anyway, most of his conversations were about animals.

'Are you okay?' I asked.

'Fine.' He gave me a kind smile. 'What about you? You seem . . . er, a little on edge.'

'I'm good,' I lied. 'What about you?'

Michael shrugged. 'I'm just a bit hot,' he admitted. 'Sometimes I wish I could thermoregulate, like a dog.'

'Right,' I said, unsure exactly what he was talking about.

We took a seat about halfway down the church, close to the aisle. I looked around. Flynn definitely wasn't here. I couldn't see any of Siobhan's family, in fact.

'So I forgot to ask your dad, how many eggs do the hens lay each week?' Michael asked, flicking casually through the order of service that lay on the shelf in front of us.

'It varies,' I said, not really listening. I'd just caught sight of Flynn's mum at the church door.

At that moment the organ started up. Flynn's mum started walking up the aisle. She stopped to chat to people along the way. When she came to me she beamed with delight.

'River, I'm so happy you're here,' she said.

'Hi.' I smiled back, my nerves suddenly vanishing. It was lovely to see Flynn's mum. I had always liked her and his sisters so much. I had been absolutely right to come here today. Flynn wasn't an issue. Today wasn't even about him. It was Siobhan and Gary's moment. That was all that really mattered.

I asked Flynn's mum how she was, but before there was time for her to answer, the organ began playing the traditional wedding march and she scuttled off to take her seat. My heart surged with the joy of the occasion as I strained my eyes towards the back of the church, looking, along with everyone else, for the bride to appear.

A cloud of white silk appeared in the doorway. Was that Siobhan? Two girls in pale green dresses were adjusting the silk. One of them looked about twenty, the other about eleven. They were both very pretty. I peered more closely at the younger girl. Was that Caitlin? The last time I'd seen Flynn's younger sister she'd been dressed in a T-shirt and jeans, her short curly hair cut in a wild bob. She looked far older than I remembered, though surely less than a year had actually passed since I'd seen her.

The two girls stood back and the white silk turned.

Siobhan stood there, looking breathtakingly beautiful, her eyes shining with excitement. She turned to someone standing behind her. He was wearing a dark suit, his face masked by her veil. I held my breath. Surely it couldn't be Siobhan's dad all dressed up and ready to give his daughter away? He was a drunk who used to beat their mum and once attacked Flynn, leaving a long jagged scar on his shoulder. He wasn't supposed to come near the family.

I waited, watching, still holding my breath. And then the figure stepped forwards and, as he took his sister's hand, I saw that it was Flynn.

3

It was him. It was really him, his dark hair longer than when I'd last seen him, his presence somehow filling the church. Flynn hadn't seen me. His eyes were on his sister beside him. She said something and he spoke back, squeezing her hand. He looked over his shoulder at the two other girls. I could see Caitlin nodding as she took her position behind Siobhan. The priest was with them now. The congregation was instructed to stand and, a moment later, the wedding group set off up the aisle.

I turned away, my heart beating fast, and bent my head over my order of service sheet. I felt faint. Giddy. I knew my face was as red as my dress.

He was here. About to pass me. I kept my head down. The music soared through a couple of chords. Then I heard the swish of silk and glanced sideways. Siobhan was walking by. Flynn was on her other side, looking across the pews nearest him. They walked to the front of the church. As they reached the altar, the music stopped. I realised I was still holding my breath and breathed in quickly, letting the air out in a shaky sigh. Beside me, Michael shuffled from side to side.

I stared at the back of Flynn's head. His dark hair was slicked back, the ends lost against the collar of the dark suit. It fitted him exactly. The older bridesmaid adjusted the long train on Siobhan's wedding dress. Flynn turned and smiled at her, then gave Caitlin an encouraging nod. He scanned the aisles swiftly, as if looking for something, then turned to face the front. Gary took his place beside Siobhan and she let go of Flynn's hand. The priest started speaking.

I didn't hear a word.

All I could hear was the sound of my own heart pounding away. A minute or two passed and Flynn and the bridesmaids sat down. Flynn was on the edge of the front row, next to his mother.

He turned around again, his eyes flickering over the people behind him, as if searching for something again. I watched his face, recognising the intense expression, the shape of his lips. It was as if no time had passed since I'd seen him. He seemed as familiar to me as my own reflection in the mirror.

And then his eyes met mine and he stopped gazing around and just stared at me.

So *I* was what he had been looking for. My heart felt so full that I thought it might burst, my blood like thunder against my temples.

He looked and he looked at me. I couldn't tear my eyes away. I had thought that after the first few dead, dark months without Flynn, my existence was more or less back to normal. But now I realised that the recent months had been dull and washed-out and that only here and now, with Flynn, was the world bursting into glorious technicolour again, everything exploding with life.

A terrible fear rose up inside me. Who had I been kidding, thinking seeing Flynn would give me closure? All I wanted was to hold him, to have him hold me, to kiss me.

I forced myself to look down. I counted to thirty. Slowly. When I looked up Flynn had turned to face the front again. Siobhan and Gary were taking their vows. Then the dark-haired bridesmaid read a poem. The priest spoke. Caitlin fidgeted. Flynn's mother wiped a tear from her eyes. Flynn put his arm around her. He didn't look around again, but I could see there was a new self-consciousness in the way he was holding himself, like he sensed I was watching him.

I felt like crying. Dad and Grace and everyone else had been right – I was back where I had been months ago, in agony. I shouldn't have come. I glanced at Michael. He had folded his order of service into a paper animal with four legs. He looked bored. I was sure he wouldn't mind if I asked him to leave.

I gulped. I couldn't just walk out in the middle of the actual wedding. But as soon as it was over, we would go. Never mind the party afterwards. I needed to get away as soon as possible.

The service was coming to an end. Siobhan and Gary were pronounced man and wife. There was a short pause while they signed the register, then the organ struck up again and the two of them came back down the aisle, arms linked, matching smiles on their faces.

Flynn followed behind. He was chatting and laughing with the twenty-something bridesmaid. Was that his girlfriend? Hot, angry jealousy filled me to the tips of my fingers. I tore my gaze away, staring down at my shoes.

As Flynn passed I could feel he was looking at me again, but I forced myself to keep my eyes on the floor.

The organ music finished and the guests headed out of the church. I turned to Michael.

'I . . . I'd like to leave now,' I said.

'You mean go home?' Michael frowned. 'What about the party?' he said.

'I'm not feeling well,' I lied.

Michael nodded, his trusting face filling with concern. 'It's really hot in here. Why don't we go outside for a moment, see if that helps you feel better?'

We headed outside. The sun was high and bright in a clear blue sky, the air warmer than when we'd gone into the church. I kept my gaze down, hanging back by the church wall. Michael disappeared to find the toilets, saying that if I wasn't feeling better when he came back we should call my dad to come and pick us up.

I closed my eyes letting the sun warm my face. It had been such a mistake to come here. What had I been thinking? Flynn was with someone else. He might still throw me an intense stare but that was probably just curiosity. Or boredom.

'River?'

My heart jumped into my throat. I opened my eyes. Flynn was standing in front of me. His green-gold eyes were almost emerald in the sunshine. There was a small scar by his top lip. He was looking down at me with a softness in his gaze that made my stomach flip over and over.

'Hi there.' The words came out all strangled: 'hghnn'.

Flynn smiled, a slow, easy grin. My insides melted.

No, this was *awful*. Everything I had ever felt for him was flooding back.

'I'm so glad you came,' he said softly. 'I told Siob she had to invite you.' He paused. 'You look the same, only better.'

I stared up at his face. There were fine lines around his eyes that hadn't been there before. His face was slightly thinner too. My head spun.

'You look the same, only older,' I said.

Flynn laughed.

The dark-haired bridesmaid appeared out of nowhere. She handed Flynn a small make-up bag.

'Look after this, will you, we're doing photos?'

'Sure. Hey, Izzy, this is River.'

Izzy smiled at me, clearly distracted. 'Hey,' she said.

She turned away. My whole being filled with jealousy again. So much for imagining I'd be able to chat easily and happily with Flynn's new girlfriend. I wanted to weep. All the feelings I'd thought I had buried were rearing up again, consuming me: jealousy . . . desire . . . love . . .

'Is that your . . . ?'

'No.' Flynn's eyes widened. 'No way. Izzy's one of Siob's oldest friends. I've known her since I was a little kid. I don't have a girlfriend.'

'Oh.' My heart leaped with joy, then with shame at

the fact that I was so pleased. I could feel myself blushing. I chattered on, trying to cover my confusion.

'Oh, I see. It's just . . . um . . . in Siobhan's note about the wedding she said you were coming with a friend?'

'Yeah, that's Cody.' Flynn indicated a tall, straight-backed boy with spiky, pale brown hair, chatting to two girls a few metres away. 'He's . . . we kind of work together.'

'Doing what?' It felt surreal to be asking Flynn such questions but in the back of my mind I was thinking that it was good we were talking like this. Small talk. It was how we needed to be now. There would be this short conversation, then I would go. And that would be that.

Flynn waved his hand. 'Stuff,' he said. 'Work's boring. Tell me about you. How's the commune? Your dad? Gemma? I heard they're having a baby.'

'That's right,' I said. 'In a few weeks.'

'What about Leo?' Flynn's face darkened slightly.

'He's fine,' I said. 'Everyone's fine.' There was a pause. 'I'm busy at school. I help out at the commune, work most Saturdays in Norton at a café.'

There was another pause. Flynn stared down at me. His presence was like a second sun, pulling me towards him, into his orbit. Dangerous. Magnetic. Powerful. He cleared his throat.

'Er, I saw who you were with in the church.' He wrinkled his nose. 'You and Michael Greene? *Seriously?*'

'Michael's nice.' I raised my eyebrows.

Flynn laughed. At that moment Caitlin came running up. She tugged at Flynn's sleeve.

'Come on,' she urged him. 'You're needed for the photos.' She glanced around at me. 'Oh, hi, River.'

'Hi.' I smiled at her.

Flynn rolled his eyes. 'I'll be right back,' he said. He looked into me, his eyes sparkling green. 'Will you wait?'

I couldn't speak. Too many emotions were crowding my head.

I nodded. *Yes.*

Flynn turned and sauntered away. I leaned against the brick wall of the church, the sun fierce on my face. I wanted to laugh and I wanted to cry. The whole world looked different, like everything had shifted a few centimetres making it all brighter, sharper, more alive.

Michael strolled up, smiling. 'There's a swallow's nest in the back bit of the church. It's up high but you can see the baby birds peeking out. I think they're getting ready to fly.'

I stared at him. His eyes suddenly registered alarm.

'River, you look really pale. I'm so sorry, I forgot you said you weren't feeling well. Did you call your dad?'

I shook my head. I peered over to the huddle of people crowded around the photographs. Laughter echoed towards us across the grass.

I had to go.

I shoved my phone at Michael. 'He's under "Dad" in my contacts list. Would you call him while I tell someone we're leaving? Tell him not to worry. I just have an upset tummy. It's nothing serious.'

Michael nodded. As he made the call I headed across the yard to the boy with the pale brown hair Flynn had described as his friend. He was watching the photo session taking place on the grass.

'Hi, are you Cody?' I said

The boy nodded. He was tall with grey eyes. He looked nothing like Flynn, though there was a similar intensity in his expression. He gazed down at me. I shivered. There was something cold and calculating about his pale eyes.

'I'm River,' I said, feeling the familiar stab of embarrassment at having to say my unusual name out loud.

Cody raised his eyebrows. 'Ah,' he said. He looked me up and down. 'River, with an R?'

'Er, yes.' I flushed, feeling like a bug under a

microscope. Why was he asking me that? 'I have to go. Will you make sure Flynn's mum and sister get the message. Say I'm really sorry to rush off. I'm . . . er . . .' My blush deepened. 'I'm not feeling well.'

'I see,' Cody said. A smile twisted about his lips. I could tell he didn't really believe I was ill.

'Bye.' I turned, feeling awkward. I walked away, on to the pavement.

One step after another, to take me away from Flynn.

I had to keep walking, I could see that now. Seeing him just brought back all the old feelings.

And I wasn't going back to those.

They'd nearly killed me once. I wasn't going to let that happen again.

4

Michael caught up with me halfway along the road. He said Dad was on his way, then insisted that as I still looked very pale we should find somewhere to sit down. I wanted to put a few streets between myself and the church, so I made him keep walking past two roads of houses and beyond the High Street, until we came to a children's playground.

I sat on a bench while Michael called Dad again to tell him exactly where we were. The playground was full of little kids, running about and playing on the swings and in the sand pit. I sat back, closing my eyes, letting the sun warm my face.

I couldn't believe how much seeing Flynn had affected me.

Michael finished speaking to Dad and went to fetch us ice creams from the nearby van. I felt too sick to eat mine, so Michael had both. I apologised for taking him away from the wedding so early. He said he didn't mind. We fell silent. I didn't want to speak. My head was still spinning, full of Flynn.

Dad arrived within twenty minutes. He must have driven fast to have got here so quickly.

'River, are you all right?' he asked, his eyes frantic with worry as Michael and I reached the car.

I reassured him I was fine, that it was just a tummy ache, that yes, I'd seen Flynn but we'd only exchanged a few words. Clearly relieved, Dad dropped Michael off and drove home.

I made a huge effort once we were back at the commune to behave normally, simply saying I didn't feel like eating. But when I went to bed that night my thoughts were, still, all of Flynn. I hadn't dreamed of him in ages but that night he paraded through my unconscious for hours, watching me, circling me, getting closer and closer – but never quite reaching me. The sense of loss, when I woke at dawn, was overpowering. I buried my face in my pillow and howled with the pain of it.

Crying helped. Once the sun was out and I was up, I felt better. It had been a shock to see Flynn, but surely the next time – if there was a next time – it would be easier.

Grace called and I told her that being near Flynn had been harder than I'd expected but that finally, after all the long months since our break-up, I was certain the relationship was fully in the past. I was exaggerating the level of closure I felt which made me uncomfortable – I didn't like not being totally honest with my friend – but I was embarrassed by how badly I'd been affected by those few minutes with Flynn. Anyway, I reasoned, it would do no good to tell Grace the unvarnished truth. She would only worry. Better to make her believe that Flynn and I were properly, conclusively over at last.

Maybe if I kept telling people that, I might start to believe it myself.

I tried to convince Leo I was fine too, but with less success. I kept away from him as long as I could, but he found me down in the apple orchard on Sunday afternoon and forced the truth out of me.

'It upset you seeing him, didn't it?' he kept insisting.

I denied it for several minutes, then finally admitted the whole encounter hadn't been easy but that I didn't want to talk about it. Leo left, looking miserable, and we hardly spoke for the rest of the week.

I took my final exam on Thursday and tried to forget about seeing Flynn. I had a busy life, I kept telling myself, full of things that weren't connected with him: my exams had gone okay, I had a social life with the handful of girls I hung out with from college and I enjoyed my waitressing job. Plus there was Grace and Dad and Gemma and my life at the commune. All these relationships and routines were important, they gave my life structure and meaning and I clung to them as the memories of my life with Flynn washed miserably over me again and again.

I made a big effort to talk to everyone at the commune as normal, listening to Dad and John's chat about dealing with the upcoming 'June drop' in the apple orchard, buying a few last-minute baby clothes with Gemma and making plans with Ros to try out some new bread recipes.

The result of all this effort was that I turned up for work at the café the following Saturday feeling like seeing Flynn had been a dream. The Rainbow Café in Norton was always busy – popular with mums during the week and families having tea out at the weekend. This Saturday was no exception. I rushed around, ferrying cakes and scones to various tables, fetching high chairs and sweeping up broken biscuits. The couple who ran the café were nice enough – though not like the lady I had worked for in London.

My shift finished at five p.m. and I was standing at the till with Mrs Anderson, the owner. She had just given me my wages when the door banged open. Flynn stood in the doorway. His hair, so carefully slicked back last week, fell messily over his face and he was out of breath, panting, as if he'd been running. He saw me and his whole face relaxed with relief.

We stared at each other for a few seconds.

'Do you know that young man, River?' Mrs Anderson asked suspiciously.

'Er, yes.' My cheeks burned as I scuttled across the café, past all the watching customers. I reached Flynn, still standing in the doorway. A breeze was whipping inside, fluttering the cloth on the nearest table.

'Are you coming in or going out?' snapped the elderly lady at the table.

Flynn ignored her. Actually I'm not sure he even heard her. He was still staring at me, his eyes – the green speckled with gold – shining with happiness.

'Thank God I found you,' he said. 'I've been looking everywhere. You said a Saturday job in a café in Norton; I've been to every single one.' He paused. 'I would have come to the commune, but I thought your dad might shoot me, so . . .'

'Come on.' I grabbed his arm and walked him out on to the pavement. The sky was filling with scurrying clouds and there was a chilly breeze in the air. Saturday afternoon traffic zoomed up and down the road. My insides were somersaulting. What was Flynn doing here? Why had he tracked me down like this?

I let go of Flynn's arm and walked along the pavement. Flynn strode beside me. He was wearing jeans and a long-sleeved top. The clothes were far less formal than the suit he'd been in last week, but still looked insanely expensive.

'Why did you run off?' he asked, his voice low and intense. 'You said you'd stay. You said we could talk. I . . . I . . .'

Fury rose up inside me. This was so typical of Flynn, full of big expansive gestures. Arriving like a storm, leaving destruction in his wake.

I stopped walking and turned on him.

'I left because it was too hard to see you,' I said. 'You might be all "Let's be friends, River, yeah? Going out was so last year, let's have a chat and catch up, blah blah blah," but I can't do that, okay? I *can't* be friends with you.'

Tears rose in my eyes. I turned away. This was awful. Humiliating. I should never have gone to that wedding. I'd been trying so hard to put Flynn in the past and here he was, larger than life, bruising back into my world again.

Bringing with him nothing but pain.

'River?' Flynn's voice sounded broken.

I turned. To my surprise tears were welling up in his eyes. I'd never seen him cry before. Well, I had. Twice. But both times before he had fought back the tears, wiping them angrily away. Now his eyes glistened and a single tear leaked on to his cheek as he spoke.

'I'm so sorry, Riv,' he said, his voice cracking. 'I just . . . it was . . . seeing you. Something . . . I can't . . . explain. I've tried to remember what you said, when I saw you last Christmas, how you're all convinced I don't love you . . . and I know that I shouldn't bother you any more . . . that you're probably with someone else. And even if you aren't, you probably don't think about me any more . . . I threw all that away . . . I hurt you. I was such an idiot.' He balled his hands into fists at his sides.

'Why are you here?' My own voice was shaking now. It wasn't fair Flynn doing this, pouring this avalanche of emotion all over me.

'I need to make you understand why I left, Riv,' he said, the tear he'd shed now dry on his cheek. 'Back last year I had to get away, sort out my head, away from college and the commune. I never stopped thinking about you or caring about you,' he pleaded. 'I *told* you. See, I still wear it, Riv.' He tugged at his top, pulling out a tiny blue R on a worn leather string. 'R for River.'

I stared at the little R, remembering the day he had put it on and how happy we had been. '"R for River". That's what that friend of yours, Cody, said at the wedding.' I took a step away.

Flynn scowled. 'Yeah, Cody guessed it was you.'

'Guessed who was me?'

Flynn stepped closer, filling up the space between us. 'The girl I've told him about, the girl from the past.' He paused, his eyes piercing through me. Then he lowered his voice to a hoarse whisper. 'The girl I'm still in love with.'

5

For a second my insides melted at his words, at the
look in his eyes. Then my anger surged back.

'You have no idea who I am any more. You're
imagining a person, imagining being in love. I'm not
the same as I was then,' I said. 'I've changed. You
don't know me any more.'

Flynn opened his mouth. I felt sure he was about
to resist what I was saying, to tell me that however I
was different on the surface, the connection between
us was still the same . . . that I could feel it and so
could he.

And I knew in my heart that this was true.

But Flynn didn't say any of that. Instead he
lowered his gaze. 'You're right,' he said. And there
was such a depth of humility and misery in his
voice that I almost wept. 'You're right, I don't
know you any more. But I'd like to, more than
anything.' He looked up. 'Will you give me that

chance, River? Will you let me get to know you again?'

I gazed into his eyes. I could just imagine Dad's anxious face if Flynn and I started seeing each other. He would hate it. So would Mum. None of my friends would understand either; and Leo – I was fairly certain – would never forgive me.

Still, it wasn't their decision. It was mine.

I could live without their respect, hard though it would be.

But I couldn't live without respecting myself.

Every cell in my body wanted to take the single step between me and Flynn. I ached to have him hold me. I longed for him to kiss me.

But he had let me down. And it was, ultimately, impossible to trust him again. We had had our time and it hadn't worked out and it didn't make any sense to think anything would be any different in the future.

I took a deep breath.

'I can't see you again,' I said. 'I understand you were mixed up last year. I get that you didn't mean to hurt me. I forgive you. But your life's a mess and—'

'It's not,' Flynn protested. 'I have a proper flat in central London. I've got a job, working with Cody. I—'

'Doing what?' I interrupted. 'I met Cody. He . . .' I

44

tailed off, remembering the cold, calculating look in the other boy's eyes.

Flynn looked away. 'It doesn't matter what I'm doing,' he said.

'No, I suppose it doesn't. I suppose all that matters to you is making lots of money.' I shook my head. 'That's all you've ever really cared about, isn't it? I mean you dress it up like you want to be the big man and have people rate you, but if you have to buy people's respect then, guess what, they *don't* respect you. Not *really*.'

I took a step away. The skies were clouding over. A few spots of rain fell. My chest heaved with emotion. Flynn stared at me, his mouth gaping in shock.

'It isn't like that,' he said. 'I mean I *am* making money, but—'

'I don't *care* about money,' I went on, feeling close to tears. It was too much, Flynn forcing me into this position. Too hard. 'Your nice clothes and your flat don't impress me and I didn't like Cody. I don't know what you do with him, but the fact that I've asked you twice and you're too embarrassed to answer tells me that it's not something you're proud of. Which makes you a bit of a loser really.' I paused. 'I'm starting to think you're destined to mess *everything* up, that messing stuff up is the person you're

45

always going to be. But it doesn't have to be the same for me.'

I took another step away. It was definitely raining now, a soft patter on my hair and shoulders. I pulled my hood up to cover my head. Flynn was still staring at me. I expected him to be angry, but he looked more upset than cross. A sense of triumph filled me. This, really, was the closure I'd been looking for. I held up my hand, palm-side out, a stop sign. 'Enough with all your big *Romeo and Juliet* feelings, Flynn. Just grow up. Try to be honest. And kind. That's what really counts.'

I turned and stalked away. Around the corner and up the High Street. I didn't look back until I reached the bus stop. I half expected Flynn to have followed me. But there was no sign of him. I sagged against the wall of the bus shelter. The rain was falling heavily now, drumming down on the shelter roof.

I felt hollow inside. Empty. Yet as if a great weight had been lifted from me. For the first time I glimpsed a future without Flynn which made me feel good.

He thought he was so grown-up, leaving college and getting whatever job it was he was doing. He thought he was big and important. But really he was small and selfish.

For the first time I felt the truth of what everyone else had been telling me for months:

46

I was better off without him.

A bus came within a few minutes. A quarter of an hour later I was back at home in the commune kitchen. Gemma was sitting at the table, sipping at a peppermint tea. She looked tired. She said she'd been having false contractions, signs that the baby would be coming soon. I made tea for myself, feeling properly happy for once. Dad and Gemma's baby meant a new life in the house, and a new life – in every sense – was exactly what I needed right now.

Another two weeks passed, Flynn didn't contact me again. Gemma's due date, when the baby was supposed to arrive, came and went. Dad was anxious, though he kept pretending he wasn't. Gemma was big and heavy and, though she never complained, I knew she was fed up with being pregnant.

Half-term was over and Leo and I were back at college for the last few weeks of the summer term, preparing for our final year at school. I went to see Mum for the weekend. We got on better now that I wasn't living with her any more. I'd moved out nearly a year before to live with Dad – and Flynn – on the commune. I was bracing myself for a lecture about Flynn. I knew Dad would have told her about me seeing him at Siobhan's wedding.

Mum was actually quite restrained, for her. She'd never liked Flynn but kept her remarks to an approving, 'I suppose it's good you've seen him just the once. Hopefully that's an end to it.'

I said nothing. I certainly didn't tell her how Flynn had pursued me to the Rainbow Café and declared he was still in love with me. I didn't tell anyone about that.

I went out on the Saturday night. Grace invited me to a party in central London with her and James. She warned me, an anxious frown on her face, that Emmi would be there. I knew she was worried that after so recently being reminded of my relationship with Flynn it would upset me to see my old friend and be reminded of her role in our break-up. But that two-second kiss with James – and Flynn's ridiculous, over-the-top reaction to it – felt like it belonged to another life now. In the past few days I'd really accepted that Flynn had been looking for a way to leave the commune anyway. Emmi was just the catalyst.

So, much to Grace's surprise I simply shrugged.

'Whatever,' I said. 'I guess I'll have to speak to her sometime.'

The party was great. James came from a rich family and had lots of well-off friends. This particular guy lived in a massive house in Camden Town and the whole place oozed money, with plenty of alcohol set on tables in every corner of a huge living room that had been stripped of furniture, like a ballroom. The walls glittered with lights and the air pulsed with music. I was surprised by how much I enjoyed it – and by all the attention I got in my dark red dress. Most of the other girls were equally dressed up and all the boys were in suits, like a prom. I saw Emmi, glamorous in a leather miniskirt and expensive-looking boots, and went straight over.

'Hey, Em,' I said.

She turned around, her eyes widening as she saw it was me.

'River.' I could see her bracing herself, ready, presumably, for me to shout at her. She knew how angry I'd been.

'It's good to see you,' I said with a big smile. 'How've you been, Em?'

Emmi's expressive face registered shock, then relief.

Then delight.

'Oh, River.' She flung her arms around me. I hugged her back. And we spent the next hour huddled in a corner, catching up.

I didn't tell her about seeing Flynn but I did fill her in on life at the commune and at sixth form college. Emmi told me about her new boyfriend

– gorgeous, apparently, but currently away at uni – and about the past few months at school.

'You were right to go to a different place for sixth form,' Emmi groaned. 'I'm *sooo* fed up. The teachers still treat us like we were in year seven. Well, not exactly, but I thought there'd be a lot more freedom than there is.'

After a while we started dancing. The whole room was moving, the entire party magical. I took a breather at one point, heading through the open glass doors and into the garden. It was a mild night and the grass was littered with couples and groups chatting and drinking and smoking. James was out there with some of his friends. We chatted for a bit. James had just finished school and he and Grace were just finalising their summer festival plans before James took a job with his dad for his gap year. 'Then Grace and I can go to uni together,' he said with a smile.

I nodded. I was happy for the pair of them but, for once, I didn't envy their relationship or their plans. Right now I felt excited at the prospect of *not* knowing what lay ahead for me.

'There's something I should tell you, River,' James started.

But before he could say anything else there was a commotion back inside the party. James and I looked in past the open glass doors as the dancing crowd parted and a new group walked through. I gasped. Cody, tall and handsome in a slim-fitting suit and shades, was striding past the dancers, a girl on either arm. Both girls were stunningly attractive – one blonde, one black, with legs up to their armpits, hair cascading down their backs and wearing the tiniest dresses I'd ever seen.

James's mouth dropped open. One of his friends whistled. My heart seemed to stop beating as Cody and his girls turned and Flynn appeared, strolling behind them, also in an expensive, skinny-fit suit, also exuding style and arrogance and also with a beautiful girl on either side.

I turned to James who was now bright red in the face. 'Is that what you wanted to tell me?'

He nodded. 'Er, River . . . I . . .' he stammered, still staring into the party room.

'It's fine.' I waved my hand and turned back to face the garden. 'I know he's back in town. You're mates. There are bound to be times when we'll bump into each other. He probably won't even bother to come over.'

'Actually—' James started.

'Hi, River.' It was Flynn.

I spun around. He must have seen me from inside the party and come straight out. The girls he'd

51

arrived with were still indoors, already surrounded by admiring guys.

'Hi.' I looked him in the eye. He might be all swagger and designer suit but I wasn't going to let that intimidate me.

Flynn grinned. 'I hoped you'd be here.'

There was an awkward silence, then James melted away. A lump rose in my throat. I wanted to say something smart and witty, but Flynn seemed to be taking away my powers of speech just by looking at me.

'Would you like a drink?' he asked politely.

'No,' I said. 'Actually, er . . . I have to go.'

I turned on my heel and headed back inside the party. Flynn didn't follow me. For a minute or two I felt shaky, ready to leave. But, then I saw Grace and Emmi across the room. Grace was laughing at something Emmi had just said. As I crossed the room they both turned and smiled and I decided that I would stay after all. Why should I let Flynn being here drive me away? Why couldn't we be in the same room? Of course it had been a bit of a shock seeing him but I was determined not to let it ruin my evening.

It's not a big deal, I kept saying to myself.

Flynn and I were over a long time ago.

6

An hour or two passed. I danced with Emmi and
other girls from my old school. I chatted with Grace
and James and a big bunch of James's friends. Every
now and then I caught sight of Flynn across the room.
He danced a little, the girls he and Cody had arrived
with writhing around him. Word had spread quickly
that all four girls were models. Most of the boys in the
room seemed ridiculously impressed.

Flynn spent much of his time talking to James – I
saw him out in the garden, a beer in one hand, a
cigarette in the other. I shook my head. When I'd
met Flynn he would never have touched either alcohol or tobacco. He was clearly avoiding me. I caught
him watching me a couple of times when we were
dancing at opposite ends of the room. He moved so
well it was hard to tear my eyes away. But I did.

I was planning on sharing a cab back to Mum's
with James and Grace in another couple of hours. I'd

told Mum I'd be home late and she'd said that so long as I travelled back with other people she didn't mind. Right now it was one a.m. and I'd been dancing non-stop for an hour. The room was packed so I decided to cool down outside. I slipped off my shoes and drifted across the lawn. The garden was enormous. I had soon passed all the couples and groups near the house and threaded my way through the trees at the back of the garden. It went on forever, not like normal London gardens at all.

Curious to see just how big it was, I kept walking, enjoying the feel of the dry, smooth grass under my toes. There was a little shed made from pale wood beyond the trees. A light shone from inside and, as I got closer, I could hear voices inside.

Raised voices.

One of them was Flynn's.

'I'm not doing it any more,' he was saying.

'Yes you are.' That was Cody. I recognised his snarl. 'You *have* to.'

'I'm pulling out,' Flynn insisted. I knew him in that mood. Whatever he was talking about, the chances of him changing his mind were slim to nil.

Cody swore. 'Man, I can't believe you're bottling it like this. I didn't think you were such a coward.'

There was a thump from inside the shed. Then another. Were they fighting? The door to the shed was open. I crept closer, keeping carefully out of sight, then peered inside.

Flynn had pinned Cody against the shed wall. Cody was struggling, the veins in his neck bulging as Flynn pressed his arm up against Cody's throat.

'I'm not bottling anything,' Flynn spat, his face close to Cody's. 'I did it at first for the money, as you know. Back then it was worth the risk. But it's over now. It's *got* to be over.'

My heart thudded. What on earth were they talking about? The way Flynn was talking made whatever he was referring to sound dodgy at the very least, if not downright illegal.

Cody said nothing. With a final shove, Flynn let go of him and backed away. Cody felt his throat where Flynn's arm had left a mark. He glared at Flynn.

'You can't just walk away.' His voice was so cold it made me shiver. 'Bentham won't let you.'

Flynn opened his mouth to speak but before he could my phone vibrated silently against my skin where I'd tucked it down the side of my dress. I jumped. And the door I was peering around banged against my arm.

The sound of wood against flesh carried – a light tap in the night air. I turned and fled across the grass.

'What was that?' Cody demanded.

Footsteps sounded across the floor of the shed. I reached the trees just as Cody and Flynn burst out of the door. Ignoring the rough twigs scratching at my bare feet, I huddled behind the nearest tree, praying it was big enough to conceal me. I could just make out Cody pacing up and down on the grass.

'Was someone there?' He ran his hand through his hair. He swore. 'I said his *name*, dammit.'

'You go that way. I'll look over here.' Flynn set off at a run towards the trees where I was hiding. Cody ran in the opposite direction.

I held my breath as Flynn entered the little copse just a few metres away from me. I could just make out the white flash of his shirt as he raced through the trees. I froze, hoping he would pass without seeing me. I didn't dare either move, for fear of him hearing, or leave the cover of the trees, in case Cody spotted me instead.

A second later and Flynn tore past. He caught sight of me and stopped. He stood, blinking, in the dim light, staring at me for a second. Then he put his finger to his lips and walked over. He bent down so his mouth was right next to my ear. I could smell his lemony aftershave and that other, Flynn-specific scent. *His* smell: sharp and male.

'Wait here,' he whispered.

He raced away, out of the trees. A few moments later I could hear him talking with Cody.

'It was just a cat,' Flynn was saying. 'I saw it jump over the fence.'

Cody muttered something in a low voice.

'I'm gonna take a leak in the trees,' Flynn said. 'I'll see you back in the house.'

Again Cody said something I couldn't hear.

'I've told you I'm quitting. I only even came out tonight because . . .' He hesitated. 'Look, it doesn't matter. I'm not talking about it any more. If he wants to have a go at me, let him.'

I leaned against my tree. My whole body felt shaky. A few moments later, Flynn was back. He stood in front of me, looking suddenly uncertain.

'Has Cody gone?' I whispered.

'Yeah, he's back in the house.' Flynn paused. 'How much did you overhear?'

I gulped. 'Enough to know you're mixed up in something bad,' I said. 'And that you're working for someone called Bentham.'

'You should forget all that.' Flynn looked away. There was a bruise around his mouth I hadn't noticed before. I reached out my hand and touched the damaged skin. Flynn turned towards me. I whipped my hand away.

'Sorry.' I could feel myself blushing violently. Why on earth had I done that? I hadn't meant to.

Flynn was searching my face, his eyes gleaming in the darkness, as intent as I'd ever seen him.

'I don't understand, River,' he said, his voice low and husky. 'From the way you brushed me off earlier, you clearly think I'm an idiot and not worth the time of day. Yet you're out here listening behind doors, looking at me like I . . . as if you . . .' He tailed off.

I shrugged. My head was spinning. It wasn't the beers I'd drunk or the shock of what I'd overheard. It was being in Flynn's presence. I closed my eyes, suddenly overwhelmed with a new longing for him. I didn't understand. I'd felt so sure I was okay without him, that seeing him earlier had just been a bit of a shock, but being here, outside and alone, felt so natural.

'It feels right, doesn't it?' Flynn's voice was even lower and hoarser than before. 'That's what you're thinking, isn't it? That you want it to be wrong, but it feels right.'

I closed my eyes. That was exactly it. I could feel the heat from Flynn's face, so close to mine. He was waiting for me to give him the tiniest signal. He was a magnet, pulling me towards him. There was no way to resist it. I tilted my face up.

The kiss shuddered right through me. My legs buckled. I leaned back against the tree. I opened my eyes. He was right there, his eyes shining.

'River.' His voice cracked and he pulled me into a hug.

I wrapped my arms around him, feeling his strong, muscular back through his jacket. We stood in silence, just holding each other.

A minute must have passed. I became aware of my phone, which had slipped as Flynn hugged me, pressing against my ribs. I suddenly remembered the text I'd received outside the shed. It was probably just Grace or Emmi looking for me, but I should check.

I disentangled myself. Flynn said nothing, but he was staring hungrily at me. I reached for my mobile where it nestled alongside the money Mum had given me for my share of the taxi home.

'Who's texting you at this hour?' Flynn said, an edge to his voice.

'Back off, Dad,' I said. 'Go and have a beer and a fag with one of your girlfriends.'

'They're *Cody's* friends, those girls we came with,' Flynn said. 'Airheads. Nothing to do with me.'

'Whatever.' I peered down at the screen. It was a text from Leo. I frowned. What was he messaging me about in the middle of the night? I opened the text: *Gemma just gone to hospital. Sounds really bad but I don't know more than that. Yr dad with her. Told him I wd let you know.*

I stared down at the screen. Gemma was in hospital? That must mean the baby was coming. It was due now. It was the right time. So why was Leo texting that things were 'really bad'.

'Something's wrong at home.' I showed Flynn the message.

A frown creased his forehead, then he looked up at me. 'What do you want to do?'

I tried to think. My instinct was to call Leo but he had already said he didn't have more information than was in the text. I could ring Dad but he was presumably busy with Gemma, which was why he hadn't called me himself. My stomach churned over. Gemma had lost a baby a year ago – an early miscarriage that I knew had upset her. This would be a million times worse. I couldn't bear to think of her and Dad not having this baby.

A sob rose in my chest. 'I want to go to the hospital,' I said.

'Okay.' Flynn nodded. 'Okay, then you're going.'

'What do you mean?'

Flynn took my hand and led me out of the trees. For a few moments I was too surprised to say anything, but as we crossed the grass I uncurled

60

my fingers from his. 'What do you mean?' I repeated, backing away. I checked the time on my phone again. 'It's one-thirty in the morning. How can I get back to Norton? It's a ninety-minute drive away and there won't be any tubes or trains running this late.'

'We'll find a way,' Flynn said, his mouth setting in that determined line I knew so well.

He was striding fast across the grass. I was almost running in my bare feet to keep up. 'I could get a taxi back to Mum's,' I said. 'Do you think she'd drive me to Norton tonight?'

Flynn shot me a glance. 'Your mum will say there's nothing you can do until morning.'

He was right.

'Then it's hopeless,' I said.

'No,' Flynn said. 'Come on.'

I followed him through the house. I couldn't see Cody though three of the girls he and Flynn had come with were still dancing. I caught sight of Emmi across the room but there was no sign of Grace and James. Flynn was already at the front door.

'Do you have a coat or anything?'

I shook my head, stopping only to slip on my shoes. I followed Flynn outside. The house was on a wide, residential street. Traffic zoomed past at the top of the road. Flynn turned towards it.

'Where are we going?' I said.

'To get you a taxi.'

'A black cab? Even a minicab will cost hundreds from here. I've only got my share of—'

'I'm paying,' Flynn said.

'I can't let you—'

He turned and pulled me towards him. He lowered his face and kissed me – a hotter, swifter kiss than before. Then he started walking again, his arm around my shoulders, pulling me with him. 'It's just money, Riv,' he said. 'You want to be there. I want to make it happen.'

I hesitated. Two black cabs passed at the top of the road. Both had their lights on. Flynn sped up. 'Come on.'

We rushed to the top of the road. Another taxi was coming. Flynn held out his arm, flagging it down. As the cab pulled over, Flynn pulled his wallet out of his pocket. He shoved the whole thing in my hands. 'Take what you need,' he said.

'*What?*'

The cab stopped. Flynn leaned in at the window, giving the driver directions to the commune. The driver baulked at first, but Flynn was insistent. At last he turned to me and opened the door.

'Get in,' he said.

'Flynn, I *can't* take your money.'

Flynn's eye bored into me. 'I don't want it,' he said. 'I was going to tell you but then . . . the way you acted before . . . I didn't think you'd want to hear it, but I'm quitting work. I'm going back to college.'

I stared at him, the night air cool on my skin.

Flynn bent closer to me. 'Everything you said was true, River,' he said softly. '*Every*thing. Nobody knows me like you.' He held open the door again. 'Get in.'

Still clutching his wallet I clambered into the taxi. I turned to Flynn, but before I could speak he slammed the door shut and the taxi sped off.

After all the noise of the party and the rush to leave it, I was alone.

7

I sat in stunned silence for a few moments, Flynn's wallet in my hand, trying to get my head around everything that had just happened.

The taxi driver was playing dance music up front. He whistled in time with the beat as he zoomed through some traffic lights. I peered out of the window. Flynn was still standing, watching me drive away.

We turned a corner and Flynn disappeared. I fastened my seat belt and opened the wallet. Inside was an Oyster card, two credit cards and two ordinary bank cards, plus a few receipts and a half-used folder of matches with the logo 'Blue Parrot' stamped on the front.

I pulled back the soft leather divider. Whoa, there had to be nearly five hundred pounds in here. What was Flynn doing carrying around so much money?

I counted out all the notes, then checked the two

remaining small pockets. One contained a condom. The other a tiny photograph that had clearly been cut from a bigger picture. I peered at it, trying to make out the face on the photo in the passing street lamps.

It was a picture of me, though I didn't remember it being taken. I was smiling in the photo, the light behind me, glowing around my hair.

I sat back and let out a long, slow, shaky breath.

The memory of our kiss in the garden filled my head. What had I been thinking?

You weren't thinking, I told myself. It was stupid. A mistake.

Well, it was also over.

Except that, at the back of my mind I knew that whatever else I did, I would have to find some way of returning this wallet to Flynn. Even if he didn't want the money, he would surely need the cards.

Trying to put him out of my mind, I texted Grace, telling her that I'd had to leave the party because Gemma had been rushed to hospital. Then I tried to ring Dad. The call went to voicemail.

My thoughts drifted back to Flynn and the argument he'd been having with Cody. What was the name of their boss? Cody had said very clearly that he wouldn't let Flynn 'walk away'.

I frowned, trying to remember.

That was it . . . Bentham.

I googled the name, then scanned past the first few entries for a philosopher, a restaurant and a railway station. At the bottom of the page I came across a newspaper report from March last year:

Lance Bentham has been cleared of killing businessman Robert Reynolds, after an Old Bailey trial lasting almost four months ended today.

Bentham, 39, was charged with murder after Reynolds, 43, was found dead at the side of a disused railway track in Acton, West London two years ago.

Leaving the courthouse today, Lance Bentham issued the following statement. 'Today's verdict is a vindication of my innocence, not just of this terrible crime but also of the ridiculous accusation that I am part of a London-based underworld. I am deeply grateful for the support of my family during this difficult time and would ask to be left in peace so that my family and I are able to get on with our lives.'

Bentham owns a chain of nightclubs and fitness centres across London and the South-East, including the popular Blue Parrot bar and the Bentham Leisure Complex.

I stared at my phone. Was Bentham a gangster? A shiver ran down my spine as I flicked open the folder of matches again. So Flynn had been to this Blue Parrot bar. What the hell had he got himself caught up in? My thoughts careered around for most of the journey back to Norton. One moment I was worrying about Dad and Gemma, the next, full of concern for Flynn. At least the roads were virtually empty, my taxi making the entire journey in just one hour and fifteen minutes, depositing me outside the hospital at 2.45 a.m. and leaving Flynn's wallet half emptied of cash.

I felt a stab of guilt, but reasoned Flynn had insisted I use his money. In fact, he'd said he didn't want it, that he was going back to college.

Did he mean that?

My head spun. I couldn't make sense of any of it. Right now, it didn't matter. Right now, all that counted was finding Dad and checking on Gemma. I headed into the hospital's A&E department and gave the receptionist Gemma's name. Unsmiling, she directed me up to the maternity ward. It took me a while to find my way but at last I arrived at the nurse's station where a harassed-looking nurse said she'd try and find Dad for me.

I sat in a plastic-backed armchair in a small waiting room near a radiator blasting out heat.

Occasionally nurses and doctors bustled past, but the place was fairly empty – and very warm. It struck me that even though I'd said I'd be late Mum might well be worrying by now, so I sent her a text explaining that I'd got a lift to the hospital. I had just finished when Dad appeared in the doorway. He looked terrible, his face pale and lined, his eyes full of worry.

I jumped up from my chair.

'Dad? What's happening? I got a text from Leo. Is Gemma okay?'

Dad nodded. He didn't speak. I went over. To my horror his eyes filled with tears. He pressed his lips more firmly together and I realised he wasn't speaking because he was trying not to cry.

'Dad?' My voice came out small and terrified. 'Dad, please, what's going on?'

'Gemma's fine, love,' he said at last. 'It was a long, long labour. They had to do an emergency c-section in the end.' He paused and pulled me into a hug. I put my arms around him, breathing in the musty, incense-scented smell of his jumper. 'How come you're here, River?'

'I . . . I . . .' There was no way I could tell him about the money from Flynn. Not while he was in this state. 'Leo sent me a text. It sounded bad, so I got someone at the party to give me a lift back here.'

Dad squeezed me tight. His body was shaking as he fought back his tears. I held him, feeling scared. I had never seen him like this before. After a moment he pulled away and blew his nose.

'Sorry, River,' he muttered. 'It's just been . . .' He shook his head, clearly unable to find the words for just how awful a night he had had.

I bit my lip, close to tears myself. 'Dad, *please*. What about the baby?' My whole body tensed, waiting for his reply.

'She's hanging in there.' Dad wiped his face. 'There was some problem, stress in the womb or something. They took her off to the neonatal intensive care unit as soon as she was out.'

I stared at him. I had a sister. He was telling me there was a new person in our family, a little girl. Despite the fact that I'd been preparing for this moment since I'd found out Gemma was pregnant, it still felt like a shock.

'River, will you go down there and see how the baby's getting on?' Dad asked. 'Gemma's in a terrible state. I can't leave her, but I hate to think of the baby being all alone.'

'Of course,' I said.

Dad disappeared. A moment later he was back, with a young nurse – all smiles and crisp, blue uniform – who took me along to the neonatal intensive care unit. I wasn't allowed in the room where the baby was but the nurse showed me through the glass window.

'There she is,' the nurse smiled.

I followed her pointing finger to one of the clear-sided cribs that lined the wall. A tiny baby lay inside, red and scrawny and wearing a little pink hat. Tubes and wires ran in and out of her body.

I gasped. 'Is she going to be all right?'

The nurse patted my shoulder. 'The next twenty-four hours are what counts.'

I stared at her. What did that mean? The nurse smiled again.

'I'm sure the doctor will give your parents an update as soon as she can,' she said.

The nurse left soon after. I stared in through the glass wall, watching my little sister. I said the words to myself: my little sister.

It didn't seem real that I was related to that tiny scrap of life in the crib. I could still feel Flynn's hot breath on my mouth, his strong back under my hands, the urgency in his voice as he propelled me into that cab.

That had been real.

I stayed in the intensive care unit for another half-hour, then Dad came and found me. He said Gemma was asleep, that he and I should go home, get some sleep ourselves, so that we could come back in the morning. As we left, he put his arm around my shoulders.

'Thank you for coming straight here, River. I don't know what I'd do without you.'

'Oh, Dad.' I gave him a hug, not knowing how to put my own feelings into words.

By the time we got back to the commune I was totally exhausted and fell asleep as soon as I lay down. I woke, hours later, as glorious sunshine poured in through the window. I lay on the bed, remembering everything that had happened last night.

Was the baby all right?

I leaped out of bed. Dad wasn't in his room. I hurried downstairs. He was in the kitchen, on the phone. As I walked in, he came off the line.

'How is she?' I asked.

'Baby's okay,' Dad said with relief. 'I'm going back to the hospital in an hour. Do you want to come?'

I nodded. In the end, the whole commune came. Not all at once, of course. We took it in turns, doing shifts throughout the day, someone to sit with Gemma, someone to keep an eye on the baby. Dad and Gemma had decided to call her Lily, a name I really liked. Gemma's parents were due to arrive that evening. They were staying in Dad and Gemma's bedroom and I was sent home at about four p.m. to

71

change the bed linen and get the room ready.

As I hauled the sheets off the bed, my phone rang. It was Grace, asking how Gemma and the baby were. I explained quickly, then Grace took a deep breath.

'I'm at James's house,' she said. 'Flynn's here too. He was worried about it all . . . about you . . . He's been bugging me since he got here to call you and find out if everything was okay.' She lowered her voice. 'Do you want to speak to him?'

I gulped. Of course I did. And yet, what would be the point? If there was one thing last night had proved, it was that Flynn and I could never just be friends. If we couldn't be together properly – and there was no way I could imagine that ever happening – then, as far as I was concerned, we couldn't be together at all.

'No.' I hesitated. Flynn had said he didn't want the contents of his wallet back but I couldn't possibly hang on to all that money, let alone all his cards. 'Tell Flynn I'm really grateful for the money for the taxi, that I'll pay him back and . . . and I'll give his wallet to James to pass on to him as soon as I can . . .'

'Okay.' Grace rang off.

I stood, a hollow feeling in my chest, Dad and Gemma's sheets still bunched in my hands.

'So you're back together, then? How lovely for

you both.' It was Leo, his voice riddled with sarcasm.

I spun around. He was standing in the doorway.

'How long were you listening?' I demanded.

Leo shrugged. His normally pale face was flushed, his slight shoulders hunched.

'I'm really wasting my time, waiting for you, aren't I?' he said.

'*Waiting* for me?' I frowned. 'Leo, we're *friends*. I thought you understood—'

'Oh, I do understand,' he interrupted. 'You and I were getting closer and closer and now Flynn clicks his fingers and you're right back where you started with him.'

'No.' I flung the sheets down on the bed. 'None of that is true.'

'Really?' Leo spat. 'Then tell me you'd care if I left the commune and moved away with Dad and Ros.'

'Of course I'd care,' I said. 'You're my best friend. At least you were until you got this stupid bee in your bonnet about Flynn. But you should be with your dad . . . and we can still visit each other. We'll always be friends.'

Leo walked towards me, his face screwed into a miserable scowl. '*Just* friends?' he said. '*Always* just friends?'

I gulped. I hated how unhappy he looked and yet it wasn't fair to give him false hope. Maybe, one day, someone else would come along who made me feel something close to the intense, amazing emotions I felt for Flynn. But that person was never going to be Leo.

'I think,' I said, trying to choose my words carefully, 'I think that if I was going to feel more for you than friendship it would have already happened. So, yes, *always*, just friends.'

Leo nodded, his eyes pale and ice-blue in the bright sunlight.

'It won't work out, you and him, you know,' he said quietly. 'It's inevitable. He is going to drag you down to his level and then he will destroy you.'

He turned and walked away. I sank on to the bed, the chill of his words running through me to my core.

Leo wasn't right.

He couldn't be right.

I wouldn't let him be right.

8

Gemma's parents came and went again, with promises to return in a couple of weeks. Dad visited the hospital every day to see Gemma and baby Lily. Gemma was fine now – due to come home soon. The baby was still poorly, but getting stronger every day. I visited too but what with Gemma in hospital and Dad spending so much time there, there was a lot to do on the commune.

Of the other residents, only two – John and Julia – were at home every day. The geeky IT guy went to work as usual and kept himself to himself. Meanwhile, Leo's dad and Ros had decided they would definitely move out – to Devon – and started taking several days at a time to tour the area, working out exactly where they wanted to set up home together.

I threw myself into A-level work at sixth form college, though not as intently as Leo. He spent hours working in the college library before, between and after all his lessons. I hadn't tried to talk to him since our argument a week ago and, as he was out of the commune so much, we weren't even travelling to and from college together any more.

After a cool spell, the weather grew hot and humid. By the end of the week the temperature was pushing thirty degrees and I was spending as much time as possible in the apple orchard, which had always been my favourite spot on the commune.

I was sitting out there under the shade of a tree on Friday after college. I had spent the past hour gathering the tiny apples that fell in the annual 'June drop'; in a minute I'd take them inside and get on with preparing that night's supper. Dad had already called to say he'd be home late.

Everyone around me was making plans for the summer. Grace and Emmi had both been on the phone, asking if I'd come on holiday with them. I said I'd think about it. But all I could really think about was Flynn.

I had taken to carrying his wallet around with me, for reasons I was trying not to examine too closely. I hadn't spent any more of the money inside, though I had examined the contents again. I hadn't heard from Flynn, either directly or through James. Despite what he'd said last weekend about not wanting the wallet back, I had to at least try and return it. The easiest thing would be to leave it with James, of course. That's what I'd told Grace I would do, what I *should* do. But the memory of my kiss with Flynn still filled my head. He'd said he was still in love with me.

I had spent the week avoiding thinking how I felt about that but, as I turned the soft leather wallet over in my hand, I knew that it was the same for me. For all my insistence that I had moved on, the truth was that I still loved him. I sat back, against the rough bark of the tree. It was a relief to admit it.

But what did I do?

One thing I knew for sure, I couldn't tell anyone. Dad and Gemma had enough to worry about with Lily still in the hospital. Mum had always hated Flynn anyway. Leo likewise. Grace would be sympathetic if I told her how I felt, but she had already made it clear she thought that seeing him again would be crazy. So had James – and he had once been Flynn's best friend. None of them really understood him like I did. Worse, none of them truly understood the strength of the emotions that still bound us to each other.

I was certain that Flynn had got involved in something criminal with that guy Bentham, but he had said – both directly to me and to Cody

– that he was ending that involvement. Didn't he deserve another chance?

Why did no one else believe in him like I did?

I sighed, thinking through my options. James was my only direct route to Flynn. But if I asked James where I could find him, he would inevitably tell Grace who would probably tell Emmi – and I'd have to face an interrogation from both of them.

I took the tiny booklet of matches out of the wallet and gazed at the Blue Parrot logo on the front. Although Flynn had said he no longer intended to work for Bentham, the people at the Blue Parrot bar – which Bentham owned – would surely know how I could contact him, as well as whether or not he'd kept his word about leaving. If he hadn't, I didn't want to see him anyway.

I decided to go to the bar and find out. I got up and brushed the grass from my jeans, feeling better for having a plan. I explained to Grace that I was going out with an old friend from home for the evening, and that if I could crash at hers that would be great. Grace was happy to agree, which meant I didn't even have to lie to Dad. In the end I left him a carefully worded note explaining that I was catching the train to London for the night, and that I'd stay over at Grace's. I felt bad that I was allowing him to assume I was spending the entire evening with her, but I couldn't see a better alternative.

Everything went as planned. Dad came home late and left again for the hospital early on Saturday morning. I did my commune chores – clearing out the hen hutch and helping John and Julia check over all the sheep. I even took on what should have been Dad and Gemma's job of preparing – and clearing – lunch, but at last I was free.

I spent quite a while in my room trying to decide what to wear. I'd checked out the Blue Parrot online and I knew it was a smart, upmarket bar. I didn't want to look out of place walking through the door. On top of that, I was still a few months off my eighteenth birthday and the last thing I needed was to be challenged about my age.

Part of me, therefore, wanted to dress up. However another part was determined that I shouldn't make too much effort in case I actually saw Flynn. It was all very well him saying he was still into me when I was wearing a slinky dress and high heels, but the real me was more likely to be found in sweatpants and trainers. If he didn't want *that* River, then he didn't really want me at all.

In the end I compromised, teaming my jeans and flat sandals with one of my favourite tops: black and silver, with a slash-neck and tiny straps on the shoulders. I shoved all the money I had into my pockets, along with Flynn's wallet, my keys, my phone and one lipgloss. Tonight, I was travelling light.

I was nervous when I arrived at the bar. It was almost nine p.m. and the place was heaving with people – though no Flynn. The place was smaller than I was expecting – and very designer. A glass-topped bar ran in a huge circle around the room. The bar staff, all dressed in black and white shirts, served from inside the circle. There were a few chairs and tables in the corners, but most people stood or sat on stools at the bar. It was hot in here and the music was loud – a love song that Flynn and I had once listened to together.

I went over to a gap in the bar and waited until one of the barmen came over.

'What can I get you?' he asked.

'Er, just a Coke, thanks,' I said. I had already decided not to drink this evening. I needed to keep a clear head.

The barman brought my drink and I fished in my pocket for cash to pay.

'Do you know a guy called Flynn?' I asked, laying a note on the counter. 'I think he might have worked here, not necessarily behind the bar, but . . . maybe out the back?'

'Flynn?' The barman shook his head. 'Sorry, sweetheart, never heard of him.' He picked up the note I'd left and turned away.

'Excuse me.' I could feel my cheeks reddening.

The barman turned back.

'Could you ask if any of the others do . . . er, please?'

The barman gazed at me for a moment. 'Is he a friend of yours?'

I nodded.

'Okay.' He headed around the bar. I watched as he spoke to first the male, then the female bar staff. He turned to find me watching him and shook his head.

My heart sank. Now what did I do? All my expectations of this evening had revolved around Flynn being known here. Still, I couldn't give up yet.

I wandered around the bar. A man – much, much older than me – asked if I'd like a drink. I shook my head and hurried on. The toilets were along a corridor to the right of the bar. I noticed there was a staff door there too but I didn't dare go through. Music thumped in the background, slightly muted here away from the bar. I was just wandering back to the hubbub when a voice sounded at my shoulder.

'If it isn't River with an R.'

I spun around. Flynn's friend, Cody, was standing

behind me. He smiled, though on his lips it looked more like a sneer. 'What are you doing here?'

I gulped. 'Er, I'm looking for Flynn.'

Cody raised his eyebrows. He looked me up and down. I shuffled from side to side, feeling desperately uncomfortable. Cody had this way of staring at me that made me feel I was being somehow undressed and ridiculed all at once.

'He's out the back,' Cody said. 'Want to see him?'

My stomach flipped over. Flynn was *here*? For a moment I felt excited at the prospect of seeing him and then I realised what this meant – that all his words about moving on, leaving his work and going back to college had been entirely empty.

'Well?' Cody demanded.

I nodded. This was my chance to tell Flynn once and for all to leave me alone. He would never change. It was time I accepted it.

A dull ache settled in my chest as I followed Cody through the staff door. He led me along a corridor, past two closed doors and a flight of stairs. A fire door was propped open at the end of the corridor. Through it I could see two men in conversation, smoking. They didn't notice us. Cody turned a corner and led me into a small office.

The music from the bar was just a dim thud in the distance now. Cody shut the door behind him.

I looked around. Apart from a wall of shelves, crowded with files, a desk with a computer and a couple of chairs the room was entirely empty.

Cody stared at me menacingly. The dull ache vanished as my heart beat wildly.

'Where's Flynn?' I asked.

'You tell me,' Cody said, walking over.

'I don't know where he is,' I said, the words falling out of my mouth as fear seized me. 'You said he was *here*.'

'I lied.' Cody looked me in the eye. His gaze was cold. He leaned closer and I could smell the stale beer on his breath. 'I haven't seen Flynn since that party last week. In fact, the last time I saw him he was heading for the front door with you. So *you* tell me where he is.'

'I don't know, I really don't.' My stomach clenched. Cody had tricked me and now I was trapped in a room with him.

Cody tilted his head to one side. 'How did you know Flynn worked here?'

I gulped. 'I didn't. I mean, I wasn't sure.'

Cody grabbed my shoulders. I gasped. He shook me. Hard. My legs banged against the desk behind me.

'You're lying,' he snapped. 'I know how he feels about you. He's talked about his mysterious ex ever since I met him. He never gave me your name but I guessed it began with R from that stupid thing he wears round his neck. It was obvious you had, like, a major hold over him. He'd say things like how great you were. How cool, how smart, how beautiful.' Cody shook his head. 'So don't expect me to believe you don't know where he is now when you were the last person to see him.'

'But I don't.' I tried to move away, but Cody held me fast. 'Let me go,' I insisted.

'Not until you tell—'

'I don't *know* where he is.' I struggled, desperate to get away.

Cody slapped my cheek.

I gasped, my hand flying to my smarting skin. Cody made a fist. He pressed me back against the desk, then raised his arm.

I shrank back as he loomed over me, his breath hot and stale in my ear.

'Tell me where he is,' he hissed, 'or I will mess up that pretty face until no one wants to look at you, not even Flynn.'

9

I stared at Cody's fist, inches from my face. Instinct took over. With a snarl I brought my knee up between his legs. He yelled out in pain, doubling over. I shoved him away from me and ran. Across the office, I flung open the door and raced away, along the corridor. The fire door was open, the two men still visible outside, their cigarettes bright spots in the gloom.

I swerved to the left, hoping to find my way back to the toilets and the bar. Another fire door. I opened it. Pushed. It clanged against the wall behind. I ran outside. Even in the dim light I could see this was just a yard, surrounded by other backyards. I could hear Cody's footsteps pounding along the corridor behind me. There was no time. I turned and raced up the fire escape. My flat sandals slapped noisily on the iron steps. I reached the first floor. The door here was open, the office beyond empty. I darted inside and stood, panting.

Silence below. I peered around the door. Cody was in the yard beneath me, looking around. I ducked back, praying he wouldn't think to come up here. My heart beat fast and loud in my ears. Music drifted up from the bar downstairs. I peered around the door again as Cody drew a gun from inside his jacket.

I gasped. I had never seen a gun in real life. Cody raised it, holding it in both hands to examine it carefully, then lowered it to his side as another man – older and balding – appeared from the building. I couldn't see his face but I was sure it was Lance Bentham. His voice was a low murmur.

'Any sign of Flynn?' Bentham asked.

'No.' Cody looked around again. 'I asked his girlfriend, but she didn't know either. She was here a minute ago, but she's gone.'

'It doesn't matter. Flynn's left. It's done. I don't want to spend any more manpower trying to find him.' Bentham sighed. 'And this is a solo job anyway.' He lowered his voice further. I could only just hear him over the steady thump of music from the bar inside. 'Got your new piece?'

Cody held up the gun and nodded.

Bentham drew a thick stack of notes from his pocket. 'Here's half the money. You get the rest when Elmore's dead.'

Dead? My breath caught in my throat. Was Cody being paid to *kill* someone? Cody gave a sharp nod.

'When do I do it?' he asked.

'Don't know yet. Elmore changes his schedule all the time. But soon.'

I stared, my eyes popping out of my head as Cody nodded again, then followed the other man inside. I realised I was still holding my breath and sucked in a lungful of air.

What the hell had just happened? I sagged against the fire door. Was Cody going to carry out a hit for money? My head spun, every cell in my body revolting at the possibility. I had to get away but I didn't dare go outside and back down the fire escape in case Cody was still nearby. Instead, I tiptoed across the room I was hiding in, past the desk and chairs and out into a dimly lit corridor. I crept along, past closed doors. Voices drifted towards me. Cigarette smoke writhed up from under one of the doors.

I sped up, my breath coming fast and hard. I reached a small staircase and raced down the steps. I stopped at the bottom, trying to get my bearings. There was a door ahead of me. I stood on the other side and pressed my ear to the wood. The music was louder here – and the sound of glass clinking and people talking. It was the bar.

I opened the door and slipped out, shutting the door swiftly behind me. Keeping my head down, I pushed my way through the crowds, past the long glass bar. The air outside was suddenly cool on my face. I turned left on to the pavement and ran. I raced on for several minutes, intent only on putting as much distance as I could between me and the bar.

At last I stopped. I was on Long Acre, close to Covent Garden tube. A taxi passed, its light on. Another was approaching. I thrust my hand out. The taxi stopped.

'Where to, love?'

My legs felt trembly. My hands were shaking. I was supposed to be going to Grace's house, but I was suddenly overwhelmed with a desire to be at home. Except Dad and Gemma weren't *at* home. Which left only one option. I opened my mouth and the next moment heard myself giving Mum's address in North London. I hadn't lived there for over a year but it was still the safest place I could imagine being right now. And Mum, for all her faults, was still my mother. I got in the cab. My hands still shook as I sent Mum a text saying I was coming, then another to Grace saying that I wasn't going back to hers after all.

I sat back, feeling Flynn's wallet in my pocket. At least I had the money to pay for the cab. Well, it was

Flynn's money but I couldn't believe he'd begrudge me spending it, not after what I'd seen.

I closed my eyes, but the image of Cody holding his gun stayed in my head. I should call the police. I didn't want to give my name but I could still make an anonymous call. The cab drove past a row of phone boxes.

'Could you pull over for a second, please?'

The driver halted the cab. I darted out, grabbed the receiver and punched 999 on the pad.

'Emergency services, which service do you require?'

I took a deep breath. 'I just saw a man out the back of the Blue Parrot bar in Soho ordering another man to kill someone called Elmore. I don't know where or when, but he said to do it soon.'

The operator hesitated. Before she could speak I carried on.

'I didn't see the first man's face so I can't be one hundred per cent sure who he is, but the guy he ordered to do the killing is definitely called Cody.'

'What is—?' the operator began.

I hung up. A second later I was back in the cab. By the time I reached Mum's I was slightly calmer. After all, I'd done the right thing in calling the police. Surely they would be able to stop Cody.

I let myself in hoping Mum would be asleep. Of course she wasn't. She was waiting in the hall for me in her dressing gown, a deep frown creasing her forehead.

'What's wrong, River?' she said.

Despite the fact that I'd *wanted* to come here, irritation rose up inside me.

'Why does something have to be wrong?' I snapped. 'I just thought it would be nice to stay here instead of going back to Grace's.'

Mum stared at me. 'It's something to do with Flynn, isn't it?'

'No,' I said. And then I burst into tears.

Mum was across the hall in a shot. She put her arms around me and I wept against her shoulder. After a moment she led me into the kitchen and we sat down at the table.

I stopped crying and blew my nose.

'What's the matter?' Mum said, leaning forward in her chair. 'Did something happen while you were out?'

I sniffed. I felt better for crying: less scared, more myself. I was upset from the shock of seeing and hearing Cody with that gun. Part of me wanted to tell Mum what I'd witnessed but I held back.

By calling the police I'd done everything I could to alert the authorities. And no one had seen me. Cody must have assumed I'd gone back to the public bar. Hopefully he had already forgotten I was ever there.

'I saw two men in . . . in a fight,' I said, choosing my words carefully. 'It . . . it was upsetting. That's all.'

Mum took my hand. 'Did it bring back memories of Flynn getting into fights?' she said, her voice oozing righteous sympathy.

I took my hand away, irritation rising again. 'Why do you always have to bring everything back to Flynn?' I demanded.

Mum looked down at the table. 'I know you still think about him, River.' Her voice was soft and low, very unlike the way she normally spoke.

I glanced away, across the kitchen. The cupboard above the sink was open. Inside I could see the coloured bowls we used for eating cereal every morning when I was little. It was weird to think I had grown up in this house. I still visited regularly, but never for very long. Mum and I just didn't get on. She had always hated Flynn – and my relationship with him.

'How do you know what I think about?' I asked.

Mum bit her lip. 'Fair enough,' she said with a sigh. 'But I do understand. More than you think. I . . .' She hesitated. 'I once . . . before I met your dad. There was someone for me like Flynn.'

I stared at her. She had to be kidding. 'You went out with someone *like Flynn*?'

91

Mum shrugged. 'In a way. Adam was older than me, twenty-two. I was your age now, not quite eighteen. He was what we used to call a drop-out . . . had a lot of dodgy friends, lived in a squat, took drugs . . .'

'That's not like Flynn at all,' I said.

'Okay.' Mum sighed again. 'I'm not saying *he* was like Flynn. Just that my parents hated him and hated me being with him.'

'Dad doesn't hate Flynn,' I said quickly. Dad had always had more time for Flynn than Mum. He'd let him come and live with us at the commune, after all.

'Doesn't he?' Mum tilted her head to one side. 'Maybe he didn't at first. Your dad has always been more trusting than me. But now?' She paused. 'After seeing you, the way you were last year, after Flynn left . . . so devastated you couldn't even speak . . . after all that, I can assure you that your Dad is every bit as angry at Flynn as I am. More, probably, because he knows he should never have agreed to have Flynn come and live at the commune in the first place.'

We sat in silence. I had never seen Mum talk about Flynn like this before – all calm and reflective. Normally the mention of his name spun her into a fury in seconds.

'I'm sorry if I've upset you, River,' Mum said, gently patting my hand. 'I know I pushed you away last year, before you moved out. I didn't mean to. It's just ... I can't bear to see you make the same mistakes I once made.'

'But you found Dad in the end, didn't you? I mean, you and Dad loved each other once.'

'Of course.' Mum smiled. 'Your father and I loved each other very much. But it was never intense like it was with Adam.' She looked away, clearly lost in her memories. 'The thing is, I thought Adam and I were meant to be. *Forever*. But we weren't. That passed, just like your dad and I passed and you being a child passed. That's the thing, River. Nothing lasts. Things you think are written in the stars can change in a heartbeat. All you can do is make the best of the time that you're given.'

It was good to get back to the commune the next morning. The fresh coat of paint we had given the main building earlier that spring gleamed bright white against the blue sky and the air smelled fresh and clear after London. Leo's dad and Ros were back from Devon, full of excitement about the cottage they wanted to buy. Dad brought Gemma home from the hospital that afternoon. Lily was out of intensive care and doing much better than before and Gemma seemed more her old self, chatting with everyone in the kitchen. She said she missed the baby desperately, but knew she was in the best place to fully recover. I agreed to go into the hospital with her the next morning for a visit on my way to sixth form college.

Mum's words echoed in my head from time to time. I also thought about Cody taking money to kill someone. Everything I'd seen and heard in the Blue Parrot seemed now to belong to some long-ago dream.

Where was Flynn? In all the drama of last night I hadn't really processed what Cody had told me – that he hadn't seen Flynn since the party. I wondered what he was doing for money. His wallet was still stuffed in my pocket. Returning it seemed impossible now.

I mused over things Flynn had said to Cody about me – how cool, how smart, how beautiful I was. And how he hadn't lied about leaving his work, even though it was clear he was in massive trouble with his boss – Bentham – for running away.

It took me ages to fall asleep that night. The image of Cody examining his gun kept flashing in front my eyes. But at last I did drift into a deep, dreamless sleep.

Hours passed. And then a creaking noise woke me. My eyes snapped open. It was still dark. I listened out. Had I dreamed the creaking sound? I turned my head.

94

A male figure was silhouetted in the doorway. I gasped, horror-struck. For a split second I stared at the man's outline, my eyes straining to focus properly.

And then he sped towards me.

10

I opened my mouth to scream. But before I could make a sound, the dark figure reached me, a shadowy blur in the dim light. His hand clamped over my mouth.

'Sssh, River.' His voice was low and as familiar as breathing.

'Flynn?' My squeak came out muffled – half relief that he wasn't a burglar who'd just broken into the commune, half shock that it was him, here, after all this time.

Flynn took his hand away. My still-sleep-filled eyes took him in. His face was pale in the dim light. 'Are you all right?' he asked.

'I think so.' I reached for my bedside lamp.

'Don't,' Flynn whispered. He sat down beside me on the bed. 'I don't want your dad to know I'm here.'

'What is it?' As I spoke, the image of Cody, gun in hand, agreeing to kill someone, forced its way into my mind's eye again. I shivered. 'What are you doing here?'

Flynn took the cardigan that hung on the chair by the bed and draped it gently over my shoulders. His hand lingered on my arm. 'I had to speak to you,' he said, taking his hand away at last and laying it on the quilt.

I touched his fingertips with mine. 'Speak to me about what?'

We stared at each other. Flynn moved nearer. 'I wish . . .'

'What?' I was locked into his eyes, pale gold in the dim light. I could feel the longing come off him in waves.

'I came to warn you,' Flynn whispered. He sat back.

My stomach clenched into a knot. 'Warn me about what?'

'Cody,' Flynn said. 'He knows that you saw him at the Blue Parrot taking money to do a job, that you called the police about it.'

The knot in my stomach tightened. 'How did he know I was there?'

'The police came round asking questions that showed they knew what had happened, though they couldn't prove it. After they'd gone, Cody checked the CCTV of the backyard. It shows the doorway of the room you were in. Cody saw you'd hidden there and he called me straightaway.' Flynn grimaced. 'To be honest, he'd been calling me since I walked out on Bentham, threatening me. I'd been ignoring him. But last night he left a message threatening *you*. So I rang him.'

'What exactly did he say?' I asked.

'That he's angry, scared you'll go back to the police, give a proper statement about what you saw.' Flynn hesitated, frowning. 'The job he was given was a hit, wasn't it?'

I nodded. 'Did he—?'

'No, he wouldn't say what had happened but it wasn't hard to work it out.' Flynn's frown deepened. 'Or to work out that he's so terrified you'll rat him out that he's going to come after you and make sure you don't. He wanted to know where you lived.'

An image of Cody's cold eyes flashed into my head. 'What did you tell him?' I whispered.

'I refused to tell him anything, but he knows your name . . . what you look like. He's met my family and some of my friends, though I've told them all to say nothing and I made sure he was on a job for Bentham miles away before I came here, so I know he hasn't followed me.' Flynn let out a despairing sigh. 'I'm so sorry, River.'

I nodded, placing my hand over his on the quilt.

Flynn curled his fingers around mine, his head bowed. A moment passed, then he looked up.

'Why were you at the Blue Parrot? Were you . . . looking for me?'

I nodded, feeling my cheeks burn. 'I . . . er, I wanted to return your money, your wallet . . .' I reached for my clothes at the end of the bed and pulled Flynn's wallet out of my pocket. I handed it to him. 'Here.'

He took the soft leather and laid it down on the bed. 'I don't want this back, I already told you. I've stopped working for Bentham and I've cancelled the bank accounts and the cards. I've got enough money to live on while I look for a proper job, but . . . but none of that matters.' He took my hand again. 'I just want you to be safe. That's why I'm here. To say how sorry I am about . . . about what you saw and to warn you to be on your guard and . . . and to tell you that I'm going to be watching over you.'

I squeezed his strong fingers, loving the touch of his hand on mine. I couldn't believe how natural, how right it felt that he was here, holding my hand. And yet what he was telling me about Cody was beyond shocking. I was in danger, he was saying, even though right here and now it didn't feel real.

'What d'you mean, "watching over me"?' I asked.

'I'll be close by, like a bodyguard, checking who comes and goes into the commune, following you to college or wherever. If you go to your mum's, I'll follow you there, too.' Flynn paused. 'I told Cody there was no way you'd go to the police, but he said you obviously already had, seeing as they'd called round to the Blue Parrot after an anonymous tip-off.'

I sucked in my breath, horrified.

'Don't be scared, Riv,' Flynn whispered. 'I'll protect you.'

'I should go to the police properly,' I said. 'I should give them my name . . . a full statement.'

Flynn shook his head. 'There's no point – you've already told the police everything you saw and heard, haven't you?'

I nodded, thinking about the man I'd seen handing Cody a stack of notes. 'I didn't give the police Bentham's name,' I said. 'I didn't see his face, you see, just that he was tall . . . and balding a bit, so —'

'It was definitely Bentham,' Flynn said. 'But if you didn't see his face, you can't identify him. So . . . again, there's no point going back to the police.'

'Right.' I hesitated. 'Bentham told Cody that he should stop looking for you.'

'Well, that's something.'

'Do you know who this Elmore is that they want to kill?'

'No,' Flynn said. 'Some other gangster, probably.'

'Has he ... Cody ... done hits for Bentham before?'

'Yes.' Flynn's voice was hollow. 'Listen, Riv, even if you can't identify him properly Bentham will be furious if he finds out you saw him – which he will if you go to the police and give a full statement. So I'm begging you not to, for your own safety. It won't make any difference to what happens. If Bentham wants someone dead, they'll be dead whether Cody does it or someone else. And right now it's just Cody who's seen the CCTV of you. He doesn't want the boss to know you witnessed their conversation because it shows he messed up. But if Bentham finds out, there's no way I'd be able to protect you. Bentham's too powerful.'

I bit my lip.

'Did you ... have you ... done stuff like that for Bentham too?'

'No, nothing like that.'

I stared at him. 'But *something*?' I persisted. 'Something illegal?'

'Yes,' Flynn groaned. 'It was stupid of me ... I did it for Mum. She'd lost one of her jobs and borrowed money from a loan shark, then the interest was ridiculous and she couldn't pay it back and Siobhan called and told me and it was the same week Bentham offered me a ... a special job...' He paused. 'I can't tell you how much I wish I hadn't agreed. I just felt so guilty that I had run away and not looked after Mum properly.'

I nodded. There was real pain in Flynn's eyes. I could totally believe he would have wanted to help his mum. He had always been so protective of her.

'I should go now,' Flynn said softly. 'The last thing we need is your dad catching me here and a whole load of questions and accusations.' He shifted away from me, letting go of my hand.

I caught it again. 'Thank you for coming to warn me about Cody,' I said.

Flynn shook his head. 'Don't, Riv, it's my fault you were even at the Blue Parrot.'

I reached up and stroked his cheek. He leaned into my hand, closing his eyes.

'I want to stay forever,' he said, softly. 'Being with you, wherever you are ... it's where I belong.'

I sighed, stroking my fingers down his cheek. 'Nobody else thinks so. They all think we're like some toxic couple, doomed, but I don't want to believe that ...'

Flynn opened his eyes. 'Like in *Romeo and Juliet*, remember? Romeo says, "then I defy you, stars" like he won't accept everything stacked against him and Juliet.'

'Right.' I made a face. 'Well, that ended well.'

Flynn laughed – a soft, unhappy sigh of a laugh. 'Oh, River,' he whispered. 'I've been such an idiot.'

There was a long pause, just the sound of our breathing in the night air. Then Flynn kissed me lightly on the lips – and left.

Light was pouring in through the window when I woke. Flynn was the first thing I thought of, but when I turned my head of course he wasn't there. He'd said he wouldn't be far away . . . watching over me.

I buried my face in the pillow. Was it wrong for me to want to be with him? I knew that everyone else would think so, that my parents and my friends would all point out that Flynn had treated me badly in leaving so abruptly and angrily last year, that he had got mixed up with dangerous gangsters – even if he'd just been trying to help his mum at the start and had broken away from them now – and that the last thing I should do was fall back into his arms.

Yet surely the truth was more complicated than that? Anyone who had seen the look in Flynn's eyes last night would realise he hadn't stopped loving me. And all he was doing right now was trying to protect me, just like he always had.

I rolled over to the side of the bed. Something glinted on the floor by the door. I sat up, then got out of bed and picked up a tiny iPod with earphones attached. A note had been tied around the earphone wire. It read: *these are my River songs – Fx*

Intrigued, I pulled the duvet over me and played the songs. They were beautiful, heartfelt tracks, some of which I knew, some of which I didn't. I listened, swept up in the music and the words. My head might argue against it, but my heart was still Flynn's. It was hopeless to resist, whatever anyone said. I couldn't have stopped myself loving him, even if I'd wanted to.

Dad came into my room at about eleven a.m., reminding me we were due to visit little Lily in hospital this morning. I got washed and dressed and joined Dad in his beaten-up car, the iPod still playing Flynn's River songs into my ears.

I looked around as we set off. There was no sign of Cody, so he clearly hadn't been able to track me down. Not yet, anyway. Was Flynn here, somewhere out of sight? How could he follow me if I was in Dad's car? Did he have a car himself? I strained looking out of the window, trying to spot him on the busy road.

There was no sign of him. As Dad, Gemma and I walked inside the hospital I looked around again but I still couldn't see him.

'What's up?' Dad asked.

'Nothing,' I said.

If Flynn was here, he was clearly keeping out of Dad's sight. Which was a good thing. Dad didn't need to be stressing about me and Flynn right now.

We made our way up to the baby ward. Lily was awake and looked so much better than when I last visited I couldn't believe the change. Up until now I'd loved the idea of her more than the reality but when Gemma put her in my arms and she looked up at me with her bright button eyes, I felt something deep inside me tugging at my emotions.

'Hello, little sister,' I murmured.

'They're saying she'll be home in just a few days now,' Gemma said, her face flushed with excitement.

'That's brilliant, love.' Dad smiled.

I stood back, looking at them both, wondering if I would ever have a family with Flynn, if our lives could ever be as simple and happy as Dad and Gemma's.

I took a picture of Dad and Gemma with Lily, then Dad took a picture of me with the baby. I immediately made it my phone's screen saver.

I spent the afternoon doing chores on the commune. Leo joined me as I weeded the vegetable patch. We hadn't spoken much since our argument. To be honest, I hadn't thought about Leo at all for days. There was too much else on my mind: what I'd witnessed at the Blue Parrot, whether or not I should go to the police about it, whether Cody was going to find me and hurt me – and if Flynn was somewhere close by right now.

'You've seen him again, haven't you?' Leo said as I dug my hoe into the rough, dry earth.

I was so shocked that I almost lost my grip, stumbling sideways over the soil. Leo caught my arm. I looked up, into his blue eyes. I couldn't bear the hurt in his expression.

'Why do you think that?' I mumbled, steadying myself and pulling away.

Leo shrugged. 'Ever since that wedding you've been different,' he said. 'Like all your lights had been out and now you've seen Flynn they're on again.'

I gazed past him, across the fields. It was comforting to think Flynn might be nearby, maybe just outside the commune.

'I'm sorry, Leo,' I said quietly. 'I don't want to talk about Flynn.'

'Fine,' he said, turning away and pushing his own hoe into the earth with a violent thrust.

We worked on in silence, and the next day, without either of us discussing it, we sat in different parts of the bus. It was ironic that Leo, who had such a difficult history with Flynn, was the only person to sense that Flynn was back in my life. I hated that he was so upset about it.

I spent the week at college in a daze. I never saw Flynn or had any sense I was being watched. He couldn't really be looking out for me all day, every day, could he? He certainly wasn't inside the college or the commune. And he had to sleep. At least there was no sign of Cody. After a few more days of worry I started to feel safe. It still niggled away at me that I should go to the police and give a proper statement about what I'd seen and heard but what was the point? Like Flynn said, I'd already told them everything I could in that phone call.

After a few days, I decided to visit Mum. A visit to London would get me away from the commune, which was presumably the first address Cody would try if he was still looking for me. And it would also give Dad and Gemma a chance to settle in with Lily. She had come home from the hospital on Tuesday and I took turns holding and changing her. She was so sweet, her face like a tiny bird's with big brown eyes just like Gemma's. She slept through the first couple of nights but Thursday was a different story. She seemed to cry off and on all night, waking me each time from what was already a disturbed sleep.

Dad was very apologetic.

'There's just not enough space between the bedrooms, River,' he said. 'I've been wondering what we'll do when she's bigger and needs her own room, too.'

It was lovely to have Lily at home but it was also a relief to know that I wouldn't be woken up all night when I went to Mum's on Friday evening. Dad drove me into London. Again, I was wondering if Flynn was watching us but, as I got inside the car there was absolutely no sign of him. And then I noticed the corner of the passenger side window. Someone had traced a tiny shape in the dust. I bent down, peering closer. It was a star.

Then I defy you, stars.

It must be Flynn.

So he *was* watching over me, after all. I straightened up and looked around. I couldn't see him but he was here, somewhere, just like he'd said.

I smiled, my heart soaring as I got into the car and we set off. Dad got me to Mum's in record time and the two of us spent an hour or so with Mum and Stone. It was nice, actually, a chance to be a family for a little bit without any pressure or rows. Stone amazed me by actually asking if Gemma and the baby were okay. He hadn't been to the hospital to visit his little half-sister yet, but Dad was taking him back to the commune for the weekend, while I spent some time with Mum.

After they'd gone, Mum fetched the Thai take-away menu so we could order in some food.

'Stone's changed,' I said.

'Yup,' Mum agreed. 'So have you.'

'Have I?' I looked at her. 'How?'

'You seem more sure of yourself,' she said. 'I don't know, maybe it's just the new baby. It makes me realise how grown-up the pair of you are now.' She looked sad for a moment.

I cleared my throat. 'Do you mind, Mum? I mean about Gemma and Dad having a baby?'

Mum sat down opposite me and put the menu on the table between us. 'No I don't mind,' she said thoughtfully. 'I mean, I wouldn't want another baby myself, but I understand Gemma . . .' She sighed. 'I guess I just feel a bit old.'

'Oh.' I wasn't sure what to say.

Mum looked up and smiled. 'Shall we order one green and one red curry?'

After we'd eaten I went up to my room to listen to the River songs again. It struck me that, for once, Mum and I had talked for over an hour without either arguing or mentioning Flynn.

I felt a sense of peace and happiness that I'd never known before. Flynn loved me and was looking out for me. And, as long as we didn't actually make contact, I could live in the delicious anticipation of seeing him soon – but I didn't have to explain the situation to anyone.

The only downside . . . the only dark cloud hovering above me . . . was that such a time couldn't possibly last.

11

I slept in late on Saturday morning, then hung out with Mum some more. Apart from the few minutes she spent suggesting I had my hair cut in a pageboy bob, whatever *that* was, Mum was remarkably non-interfering. She put up no resistance to my suggestion that I might go over to see Grace that evening and seemed pleased when I told her I was on friendly terms again with Emmi.

I didn't leave the house all afternoon but I did look around when I set off to walk to Grace's that night. There was no sign of Flynn – or of Cody. I wondered if Flynn would really have followed me to London. After walking to Grace's house and there still being no sign of him, I was convinced he couldn't possibly be here. I mean, surely he would come up to me if he saw me on my own?

Grace cooed over my pictures of Lily, then she and I spent a fun hour getting ready to go to a party.

This one was in central London – and being given by another friend of James who Grace appeared to know quite well but I'd never met. Emmi and some of my other old friends from school were coming too. Grace and I were just finishing our make-up when James arrived. I could see something was wrong as soon as he walked in, though Grace – flying into the bathroom – didn't notice.

'What is it?' I asked as soon as she'd shut the door.

James frowned. 'This guy's been asking about you, River. A friend of Flynn's, Cody Walsh. He was at that party we all went to last week.'

My insides shrivelled. 'Cody Walsh?'

James nodded. 'He turned up at my house a few days ago, demanding to know where you lived.'

I gasped. 'What did you say?'

'Nothing.' James made a face. 'Flynn had already called me, warned me the guy was dangerous and that I shouldn't give him any information.'

'Did he say why Cody wanted to find me?'

'No.' James shrugged. 'But Flynn was adamant I should say I didn't know your address.'

'Thanks.' I sank down on to Grace's bed, my head in my hands. The whole idea of Cody trying to trace me had started to seem a little far-fetched but now here was James confirming exactly that . . . exactly what Flynn had warned me of a week ago.

I shivered.

'I'm sorry, River,' James said. 'What happened? Cody didn't seem that odd to me at the party, but Flynn made him sound like a psycho.'

I gulped. I couldn't tell James the truth. 'I think he got the wrong end of the stick about something,' I said vaguely.

'Well, don't say anything to Grace, will you?' James urged. 'I don't want her getting all stressed.' He shook his head. 'Trouble follows Flynn everywhere, doesn't it?' he said wearily. 'Look, River, you know I like him, yeah? Flynn's a great guy. He stands up for himself and he's loyal to people and . . . and he does really love you. He knows he made a mistake getting involved with a gangster and he's trying to deal with all that. But honestly, you are so much better off not having anything to do with him. Or people like Cody Walsh.'

'Right,' I said, as Grace came back into the room. Was James right that I should back away from Flynn? After all, it wasn't directly Flynn's fault that I'd witnessed Cody being paid to kill someone . . . or that Cody was now trying to track me down.

An hour or so later we arrived at the party. For a while I actually managed to enjoy myself, catching up with a few friends from my old school and putting thoughts of Cody out of my head.

Then Emmi cornered me.

'What's going on with Flynn?' she said, her eyes sparkling with mischief. 'Grace didn't notice but *I* saw the two of you leaving that party last week. Are you having a thing for old times' sake?'

I could feel myself blushing. 'Flynn was just helping me get a taxi home,' I said.

'Yeah, right.' Emmi raised an eyebrow. 'Come on, girl, *talk* to me. After all this time, you wouldn't really go there again, would you?'

I bit my lip, unwilling to lie, unable to tell the truth.

The smile on Emmi's lips faltered. A look of consternation came into her eyes. 'Oh, I'm sorry if I've put my foot in it. I didn't mean to upset you.'

'You haven't. I'm not seeing Flynn. Seriously. He did help me out last week, but that's it. I haven't seen or talked to him since last weekend.' I looked Emmi in the eye, feeling a blush creep across my cheeks. Everything I'd said was true in the strictest sense, of course, but I couldn't help but feel uncomfortable saying it.

Emmi blew out her breath. 'Well, that's a relief. I thought for a moment you were going to say you were going back out with him. But even you wouldn't be that crazy.' She laughed.

'Right,' I said.

We chatted away for a bit but I felt hollow inside. Why was it so hard for everyone to understand that love wasn't a switch you could flick on or off. Suddenly, in the middle of the heaving party, I felt totally alone. I wandered outside, to the front of the house. Two guys were smoking. They glanced at me, then carried on their conversation. Feeling self-conscious, I wandered to the end of the road. It was late, but London was still full of lights and bustle. I looked around. There was absolutely no sign of Flynn. I felt more depressed than ever.

The traffic died down as I walked around the block. I just needed a little time to psych myself up before going back into the party. The wind whipped around the corner of a tall office building. It wasn't a cold night but I was only wearing a short-sleeved dress with bare legs and I shivered.

And then a man strode around the corner up ahead of me. He was walking intently towards me, his head down. I stopped walking and stared at him. Was that Cody?

He was about the same height and dressed in a similar silver-grey suit to the one I'd seen Cody wearing. I hesitated. The man strode towards me. He was getting closer and closer. Why didn't he look up, so I could see his face?

Panic seized me. I turned and ran. My heels

115

slowed me down, but I pushed myself on. As I reached the end of the road I looked over my shoulder. The man in the suit had vanished. Had he gone? Or was it Cody, hiding . . . waiting to sneak up on me?

I couldn't think clearly. All I knew was that I had to get away. I plunged down the next street, past more deserted office buildings, then stopped to get my bearings. I took a deep breath and headed back to the party. As I turned around the next corner, I ran into a group of men. They were staggering along, clearly drunk and laughing and shouting at each other.

'Excuse me.' I tried to walk past the man at the end of the group, but he grabbed my arm.

'Come with us,' he slurred.

'No.' I tried to pull away.

The other men were moving past us. One of them called out, 'Leave her alone, you big perv.' The guy holding my arm yanked me closer towards him.

'Don't you want a drink, love?' he said.

'No.' I tugged my arm out of his grip, but before I could move on, a figure flew past me, so fast he was almost a blur. Flynn shoved the man in the chest.

I gasped. So he *had* been here, watching over me after all. The man he had pushed roared out. His friends turned.

116

'Hey!'

'Oy!'

'Stop it!'

The shouts rose up.

Flynn took my hand. His eyes met mine.

'Run!' he said.

12

We tore down the street. Flynn was gripping my arm so tightly I practically flew along beside him, half off my feet. I could hear footsteps behind us, but there was no time to look over my shoulder.

A hand grabbed my hair. I was yanked back, torn in two directions by the man who was gripping my hair and Flynn, who hadn't let go of my arm.

'You shouldn't have pushed me,' the man snarled.

'You shouldn't have touched her,' Flynn snapped back.

'Let me go,' I demanded.

The man released my hair. He was older than us, in his thirties at least, and tall and thickset. Flynn drew me behind him as the man's friends jogged up. They surrounded us. My heart raced. Never mind Cody, this was real danger, right here. I glanced at Flynn. He was standing, squared up to the tall man with his fists clenched. Flynn was muscular himself, but this guy was far bigger and looked much stronger.

'Please, just let us go,' I said quickly.

The man ignored me, but Flynn looked over, concern spreading across his face. He took a step away, opening his hands in a gesture of surrender.

'I don't want to fight,' he said.

I stared at him. I had never, ever, in all the time I'd known him seen Flynn willingly back away from an argument.

'Let them go, Paul,' one of the men nearby said with a grunt. 'They're just a couple of kids.'

'Yeah, and you *were* hassling her,' said another.

Paul sneered at Flynn, ignoring his friends. 'Don't fancy your chances? Think I'd take you?'

Flynn's fists clenched again. But, as before, he glanced at me, his face creased with doubt. He hesitated a second then said:

'I just want my girlfriend to be safe.'

I stared at him.

'That's fair enough, Paul,' said the man who'd spoken before. 'Come on, don't be a jerk.' He put his arm around Paul's shoulders and steered him away.

The others all followed.

Seconds later the pavement was empty, as if the whole incident had never happened. A gust of wind blew a carton of juice across the path ahead of us. It scratched against the concrete, the only sound suddenly apart from the distant hum of traffic.

Flynn stood in front of me, his head bowed. The bruise I'd seen last week had faded from his skin, but his face still seemed thinner and older than I remembered from last year.

'I'm sorry I called you my girlfriend,' he mumbled. 'I just thought it might help them leave us alone.'

'You backed down,' I said.

Flynn shrugged. He still hadn't looked up at me. 'What mattered was, well, what I said . . . keeping you safe. A fight with so many people wasn't going to do that. I'm sorry if it wasn't the right thing to—'

'It was,' I said. 'Though that guy deserved a slap.'

Flynn smiled. He looked up at last, his eyes meeting mine, full of longing and hurt and love.

My guts tumbled and twisted inside me. 'You were here,' I said. 'Watching over me, like you said.'

'I have been since I saw you. I *promised* I would and I have. I've been hiding out of sight near the commune, watching who comes and goes. I've got a car. I've only slept when I'm sure you're safe.' He blew out his breath.

'Next you'll be saying you've stopped smoking.' I laughed.

'I have,' he said, moving closer. 'You said you didn't like it, so I've stopped. I only started because . . . well, it was like the drinking. I realised that what I'd been doing before – not ever touching any alcohol – I was trying to be the opposite of my dad, but it was stupid – that way he was still controlling who I was . . . I mean why shouldn't I have a few drinks? It doesn't make me him.' He ran his hand down my bare arm. His touch sent a shiver running right through me. 'I'm here,' he whispered. 'On any terms you like. All I want to do is make sure Cody doesn't find you and hurt you.'

I bit my lip, trying to ignore the delicious feel of his fingers on my arm. I moved slightly away. 'I feel bad not going to the police and telling them properly about Cody agreeing to do the hit. You know, giving my name, making a statement.'

Flynn frowned. 'I don't think it'll make any difference, but I'll back you, whatever you want to do. All I'm asking is for you to let me carry on watching over you. If Cody hasn't found you in another week or so then I'm guessing he'll calm down. Maybe he already has, but I want to be sure you're all right.'

'I thought I saw him earlier – there was a guy in a silver-grey suit. That's why I ran.'

'I saw him, it wasn't Cody,' Flynn said, meeting my gaze again.

'You were watching me the whole time?'

'Yes.'

I wanted to ask Flynn why he hadn't come up to me when I was alone just now or when I was walking between Mum's and Grace's houses earlier this evening, but suddenly the question felt too exposing. It would show I cared, that I wanted him to be with me. And, after everything that had happened between us, I didn't want to be that vulnerable in front of him.

Flynn took my hand, clearly sensing what I was thinking. 'I wanted to come and speak to you before. I *want* to be with you, River. But it's not fair. I mean apart from that probably being the last thing you really want, if we were together again you'd have to deal with everyone else being angry or upset – your friends, your parents. I get that.' He squeezed my hand. 'Still, as I'm here now I could walk with you back to the party?'

'Sure.'

We set off along the pavement. My head was spinning. On the one hand Flynn was saying that he wanted to be with me again. On the other, that he was planning on keeping his distance . . . for *my* sake, so that I could stay in this limbo place where I didn't have to deal with the reality of a relationship and all the fallout it would bring.

I stopped walking and took a deep breath. 'Do you want to go out with me again?'

Flynn frowned. 'River, I already told you, I want

to be with you for the rest of my life. I always have – I just didn't used to believe I deserved you.' He looked away. 'I still don't really.'

I stared at him.

'I know it's not supposed to happen to people when they're young,' he went on. 'But it's happened to me. I *know* it. You're the only person I'll ever truly love. *That's* what's in the stars, not what all those other people think.'

We stood in silence again. My heart thudded.

'I feel the same.' My voice came out as a tiny whisper.

'Oh, Riv.' Flynn drew me towards him and we hugged.

It was so good to be in his arms. I breathed in his scent, his shirt soft against my cheek, his chest firm and muscular underneath. Then I pulled away and placed my hands on his face.

'I want to be with you,' I stammered. 'But so much has happened. And you *left* me. I get that you were all upset and confused last year, but you still handled the situation really badly. And you got involved with Bentham, maybe at first because you were trying to help your mum, but you *stayed*. You might have taken the first bit of money for her, but I can see the clothes you're wearing and—'

'Bentham wouldn't let me leave,' Flynn interrupted.

'After the first job I wanted to stop, but he said I had to do one more so I said yes, but of course after I'd done one more, there was another. Then another. I'd think he was finally letting me alone, then Cody would say I was needed again. In the end I realised he was never going to let me go, so I got out.'

'What did these jobs involve?' I asked. 'What kind of work did you do for him?'

'I was just his bodyguard at first, but the jobs were different . . .' Flynn hesitated. 'It's complicated. I was never involved in any real violence. I hate talking about it. I feel so stupid that I got suckered into the whole thing in the first place.'

I nodded. 'That's part of the problem though, don't you see? I don't know who you are any more – I mean I don't know what you've been through and how your life has been. And I've changed too.'

'So you're saying we need to get to know each other again?' Flynn asked, his intelligent eyes burning with intensity. 'I can do that. We can do it.'

'Yes,' I said, thinking about what he'd said. 'And getting to know each other means taking it slow, not leaping into a relationship or . . . or . . .'

'Or a bed.' Flynn laughed. He drew me close and hugged me again. 'I agree. It sounds brilliant. I'll do whatever you say, take it as slow as you like.'

We started walking again, our arms around each

other. I felt happier than I had done for ages, yet somewhere deep inside me I was anxious too. What would everyone say if they knew I was seeing Flynn again? However slowly we took it, most of my friends and certainly both my parents would be appalled that I was letting him into my life once more. Not just because he had hurt me so badly before, but because he was mixed up with murderous gangsters, one of whom was now trying to hunt me down.

But Flynn had only gone with the gangsters to try and help his mum and he'd only hurt me because he was a mess last year, not because he meant to be cruel or because he wanted someone else. He'd left Bentham, so he was trying to put that mistake behind him. And he still loved me. He always had.

'How are we going to do this?' I said, leaning into him as we turned the corner on to the street where the party was being held.

'However you like,' Flynn said softly. 'Maybe I could see you tomorrow? Take you out for tea?'

'Take me for tea?' I laughed. 'You make us sound about ninety.'

'Okay, then tell me what you want,' Flynn said. 'And we can do it next week or next month if tomorrow's too soon.'

'You'll wait?' I asked, gazing up at him.

'Yes,' he said. 'Forever.'

We were just a few doors away from the party house now. I glanced over. No one was outside. I reached up and kissed his lips.

His mouth opened hungrily and soon I was lost in a burning kiss, my whole body melting into him.

It was several minutes before we finally stopped and I drew away. Flynn rubbed his forehead. His face was flushed, his eyes lit up. I filled with delicious pride that I had such an effect on him.

He looked up and shook his head. 'Kissing you, Riv, it's not like anything else in the world.'

'Good.' I smiled. 'So tea . . . tomorrow?'

Flynn nodded eagerly. 'Where? Will you be back in Norton by then?'

'No,' I explained. 'I'll still be at Mum's. Dad isn't picking me up until evening.'

'Okay, so somewhere near your mum's then?'

We stood talking for a moment, fixing on a time and a place, then we kissed once more and Flynn let me go. 'Don't forget I'll still be watching over you,' he called out softly as I walked away.

I went back into the party and wandered through the throng of people dancing, one minute thrilling with excitement at the memory of our kiss and the prospect of seeing Flynn properly tomorrow, the next full of anxiety about how going out with him again could possibly work.

Well, I wasn't going to worry about that now. Tomorrow was just a toe in the water, a chance to see how we were outside all the drama of Cody and the debris from our previous relationship.

I saw Grace and James dancing in a group and headed over. For a moment I wondered where Flynn was right now. Was he really outside? Standing guard over me somewhere close by? Hidden from everyone in here? Then I let the music take over and got lost in the dance.

It was fun. More fun now that I knew where I stood with Flynn. I was actually surprised when Grace leaned over and said it was nearly 2.30 a.m. and she and James were going to go home and did I want to share a cab?

I agreed, somewhat reluctantly. Still, once I was safe back at Mum's at least Flynn would hopefully get some rest from being my bodyguard.

Grace went to say goodbye to someone while I waited with James at the front door. As I stood there, Emmi wandered over. She looked a bit tipsy, her lipstick smudged.

'Can I have a word, River?' she asked.

'Sorry, Em, we're leaving,' I said. 'Do you want a lift with us?'

Emmi shook her head. She narrowed her eyes at James, who took the hint and backed away.

As soon as he was a few metres across the room, Emmi leaned in close, whispering in my ear. 'River,' she said urgently. 'What's going on?' Despite that smudged lipstick, she didn't sound drunk at all.

I frowned. 'What do you mean?'

Emmi lowered her voice. 'I saw you outside, walking up the road with Flynn.' She narrowed her eyes. 'You were kissing, like . . . like you were *totally* back together, but you said you'd hardly seen him. What's going on?'

I stared at her. Of all the people in the world, Emmi, who had betrayed my secret about James and the nano-kiss to such devastating effect last year, was the last person I would have chosen to confide in.

'We're not back together,' I said, looking her straight in the eye.

Emmi snorted. 'That's not what it looked like.' She paused. 'Don't worry, I'm not going to tell anyone, River. I learned my lesson about butting into other people's business last year. So your secret is safe, but . . .'

'There's no secret,' I hissed. 'I keep telling you, we're not back together, just . . . just . . .'

Emmi tilted her head to one side. 'You can only kid yourself for so long, River. Just remember who you're dealing with. It's *Flynn*. It won't end well. It never does with him. You'll be hurt. *Again.*' She sighed and when she spoke next, her voice was more serious than I'd ever heard it. 'It's much more dangerous than when he was just a bit of a rebel at school. He's mixed up with really bad people and he'll end up destroying you if you're not careful.'

'You don't know what you're talking about.' Fear and anger swirled in my guts. 'He's left those people.'

'It's not that easy.' Emmi shook her head, as Grace ran over.

'Sorry,' Grace said. 'I got chatting.' She looked at us. 'What's up?'

'Nothing,' Emmi said quickly. 'I'll see you guys soon.'

She went back into the party and Grace, James and I headed outside. As we walked towards our cab, Emmi's words about Flynn 'destroying' me echoed in my head. Leo had said almost exactly the same thing to me the other day. Emmi and Leo were about as different from each other as it's possible for two people to be and yet they both thought Flynn was destined to ruin my life.

It was ridiculous. Melodramatic. Wasn't it? Didn't the fact that he wanted to change, *had* changed, count for anything? Didn't our love for each other make a difference?

We reached the taxi. Before I got inside, I looked around trying to spot Flynn but I couldn't see him. A couple of minutes later I felt my phone buzz. It was a text from a number I didn't recognise. From him.

Hope ok to txt. Get home safe. C u 2mro x

I shut my phone and stared out at the London lights which gleamed and blurred as we passed through busy streets. James and Grace were chatting happily about the party but I couldn't join in.

Nobody understood me and Flynn. Nobody was ever going to. If we were going to be together, I had to accept that.

There was no alternative future except one in which I was without him entirely.

And that was not a future I could accept.

13

Flynn was waiting when I arrived at the café the following afternoon. It was raining and I'd been hurrying along the street, pulling my hood over my head so that my hair wouldn't get wet and frizz up. I'd been looking around the whole way, wondering where he was. Despite my attempts to spot him, he stayed out of sight until I got there, when I saw him at last on the other side of the road.

He waved, then darted through the traffic and rushed up to me.

'It's our first date all over again,' he said.

I grinned as we went into the café. This was, indeed, the first place we had ever come on our own together. Back then, almost two years ago, I'd bumped into him on the Broadway with his sister, Siobhan. He had dropped her at the hair salon where she worked, then asked me if I wanted a cup of coffee. We hardly knew each other back then, just a few weeks into the rehearsals for *Romeo and Juliet*.

'That wasn't really a date,' I said, as Flynn led me over to the same table where we'd sat on that first occasion. 'If I remember correctly you were really rude to me.'

'Oh, yeah?' Flynn pulled out a chair for me. 'I think you were pretty rude yourself. You asked me why I was so bothered about being poor.'

'Only because you bit my head off when I offered to pay my share of the bill.'

Flynn made a face. 'Yeah, you're right, I did.' He sighed. 'I was a bit of a jerk about money back then.'

'A *bit*?' I raised my eyebrows.

Flynn grinned, then bought our coffees. I asked for a cappuccino, just as I had back then. Flynn ordered a plain black coffee. He brought them back to our table and sat down.

'So,' he said. 'Let's start again.' He cleared his throat. 'It's nice to meet you, River. Thank you for agreeing to go out on a date with me.'

I giggled. 'Um, well, I thought I'd give you a try, see how you handled my questions.'

'Questions? Okay.' Flynn took a gulp of coffee then set his cup back in the saucer. 'Ask away,' he said. 'Three questions, then it's my turn.'

'Fine.' I narrowed my eyes. 'My first question is

how you are managing to follow me everywhere without me seeing you?'

Flynn's face broke into a huge grin. '*That's* your first question?' He laughed. 'It's simple. I stay far enough away to be hidden, but close enough to see you.' He lowered his voice. 'When Bentham took me on to his security staff, he trained me to get in and out of places quietly, so I could move around without drawing attention to myself.'

'Did he teach you to use a gun, too?'

Flynn looked down at the table between us. I was suddenly aware of the buzz of the café, the chattering voices all around, and us here at the table inside our own intense little bubble.

'I told you, I've never been involved with any real violence and I've never used a gun.' Flynn spoke so softly I could barely hear him. 'But I know Bentham does. And Cody.'

I took a deep breath, then leaned closer towards him. 'Has Cody killed anyone before?' I whispered.

Flynn met my eyes. 'I don't know for sure. I mean, I don't know any details but I think so, yes. But not me, Riv, you have to believe that.'

I stared at him. There was something he wasn't saying. 'What have you done then?' I asked.

'You've had three questions,' Flynn said, looking down at his coffee. 'It's my turn.'

'No,' I said. 'I think I'm entitled to an answer. Explain it from the beginning ... how you got involved with Bentham ... *everything*.'

There was a long pause. 'Okay,' Flynn said. 'Well, it all started about a week after I left the commune. I'd gone to Manchester because I couldn't bear to be in London. A guy I used to work with at Goldbar's had fixed me up with a job as a bouncer in a night-club. Bentham came in one day. Some drunk slipped past his bodyguard and tried to punch him. I stopped the drunk. Bentham was impressed. He told Cody to take me on. Cody and I hit it off at first, but then everything went wrong ...' He blew out his breath.

'Go on,' I said.

'So ... at first I just worked as a bodyguard, no weapons, just muscle. I did that for a month or so and it was well paid, but I had no idea who Bentham really was. Then we came back to London which is where Bentham is based and I started to realise that some of the business things he was doing were probably dodgy, but I thought it was more to do with fraud not violence. Anyway, it got to February or so and Siobhan had called to say Mum needed money and I'd been sending her cash but I didn't have enough to cover what she owed and just at that exact moment, Cody asked if I wanted to earn some extra cash. A *lot* of extra cash. All I had to do . . .' he lowered his voice, '. . . was hide a gun for Bentham. He moves them about because it's illegal to own them but he needs them nearby to protect all his money. So . . . so I stashed a revolver for him in my flat.'

'But that's . . .' I covered my mouth with my hand.

'Illegal . . . stupid . . . dangerous . . .' Flynn rubbed his forehead, then took a long swig of coffee. 'I know.' He set his cup down again. 'I did it for the money for Mum. I thought that would be it, but of course Bentham got all heavy and threatened me if I didn't do it again. Which I did because I was scared.' Flynn sighed. 'I can't tell you how much I regret having anything to do with Bentham or Cody or any of them.'

I sat back and sipped at the froth on my cappuccino. In a way, my worst suspicions had been fulfilled. Flynn had been breaking the law. Bentham was an out and out gangster, Cody almost as bad. And yet I believed Flynn when he said he'd never actually used a gun himself.

'Can I ask *you* something now, River?' Flynn hesitated.

I nodded, my mind still on everything he'd told me. 'Go on.'

Flynn leaned forward. 'Tell me . . . what do I

135

need to . . . how can I make up for everything I've done wrong? I hurt you by running away. I was a coward. I never stopped loving you, but I didn't . . . couldn't do the grown-up thing and just talk it through. So now, after all that, what can I do to make things better?'

I gazed into his expressive eyes. All his emotions were there: hurt and anger and love and longing.

'The more time that passes,' Flynn went on, 'the more I realise just how stupid I was to overreact about you kissing James. It was never really about that. I was . . . it was my whole life, feeling I didn't know who I was or what I wanted. So . . . so how do I say sorry now?'

I shrugged. 'I don't know,' I said truthfully.

We sat in silence for a bit.

'I need to be able to trust that you won't fly off the handle,' I said at last. 'That's one thing.'

Flynn nodded.

'And you need to be honest with me,' I went on. 'You need to tell me how you're feeling, what you're going through.' I paused. 'Are you really going back to college?'

'Yes, I'm going to retake this whole year. Maybe not at Norton, but somewhere nearby, so I can see you every day. It'll mean we'll be in the same year, so we can apply to college together.'

'Do you still want to do Law at uni?' I asked.

'No, History. I've decided I don't want to be a lawyer. But History is interesting and doing a degree will give me a chance to work out what comes next.'

'Wow.' I drank some more of my cappuccino. 'You sound determined.'

Flynn smiled. 'Once we're sure Cody has calmed down, then I'll look for a place to stay and a job.'

'Where are you living now?' I asked.

'In my car,' Flynn said.

'*What?* You can't sleep in your *car*. When did you learn to drive, anyway?'

'Earlier this year.' Flynn smiled at the look of horror on my face. 'I got the car with some of the money I made. I was going to get rid of it, but right now I need it to help me watch over you. Honestly, Riv, it's cool. I drive around when I know you're safe, take thirty-minute breaks, go to where I can get a wash, do my laundry. Once I find a flat I'll sell the car for the deposit and look for a proper job.'

'Sounds like a great plan,' I said drily. 'My mum and dad would be impressed.'

'Don't,' Flynn groaned. 'I know they hate me.'

I made a face. 'Let's not talk about them now. We can work out what to say to them another time.'

Flynn finished his coffee. 'Can I walk with you up the road for a bit? My car's parked around the corner. And . . . and maybe we could fix our next date?' He hesitated. 'I was wondering if it would be okay if I called you as well?'

'Yes.' I stood up. A few calls and texts and another date didn't amount to a proper relationship, just as loving each other wasn't enough to make that relationship work. I needed to find out if I could trust Flynn again, and that would only happen over time, after we'd done a whole bunch of small, ordinary things together, away from all the drama of everything that had happened with Cody. And away from other people's fixed opinions. Because Flynn was right that Mum and Dad would hate me seeing him, but in the end it was my life, nobody else's business.

Flynn and I left the café. It was still raining, and Flynn put his arm across my shoulders as we hurried up the Broadway and into the shelter of a doorway.

'We should say goodbye here,' I said. The closer we got to home, the more danger there was of someone I knew seeing us. 'Thanks for a lovely first date.'

'Thank you,' Flynn murmured, then he took my face in his hands and drew me into a long, sweet kiss.

Eventually I pulled away. 'That wasn't a very "first date" kiss,' I said.

Flynn's eyes twinkled. 'Let me try ag—'

'Hey!' A rough hand grabbed my arm. I gasped.

It was Cody. He stood beside us, his hair damp against his face, one fist thrust into the pocket of his jacket, the other still holding my arm.

'Get off me!'

'Let her go!'

Flynn and I spoke at once. Cody ignored us. He fixed his eyes on me.

'My gun is pointing right at you, River,' he muttered. 'If you don't come with me now, I'll shoot.'

'What?' Panic rose inside me.

'What the hell are you doing?' Flynn demanded.

'Back off.' Cody swore. 'It's River I need to speak to.'

'*Please*,' I said, my voice a hoarse whisper. '*Please*, I prom—'

'Shut up.' Cody moved closer, prodding me with the gun in his pocket.

He glanced at Flynn. 'I only want to talk to River for a moment, okay? Walk away.'

With a desperate look at me, Flynn took a couple of steps back. Cody grabbed my arm and dragged me across the pavement. I wanted to shout out, but fear kept my scream in my throat. We reached a sports car. Cody opened the passenger door and shoved me inside. As he raced around to the driver's seat, I looked in the wing mirror. Flynn was pelting along the road. I peered more closely, watching as he stopped running and got into a car himself. I caught a flash of a door slamming, then he was out of sight.

Cody jumped into the car beside me and before I knew what was happening, we had roared away.

14

The car sped along. Within seconds we were zooming fast, heading across the roundabout and towards the main road. I shrank back, into the corner of the passenger seat.

'What are you doing?' I found my voice at last.

Cody glanced across at me. His gun was in his lap. Beads of sweat glistened on his forehead. 'I just need to talk to you,' he muttered.

'*Talk* to me?' I shook my head. Panic swirled in my guts. 'We could have *talked* on the pavement. You didn't have to force me into a car at gunpoint.'

Cody said nothing.

'What are you going to do with me?' My heart was beating so fast I felt sick.

'I had to get you away from Flynn,' Cody said. His hands gripped the steering wheel, his eyes darting over the road ahead.

I glanced into the wing mirror again. Was Flynn

behind us somewhere? I cursed myself for not having asked him about his car. I'd only seen a flash of the door as it shut. I wasn't even sure what colour it was, so, unless it was right behind us, I wouldn't be able to spot Flynn at all.

'Come *on*.' The traffic had slowed up ahead. Cody swore at the stationary cars. He looked seriously unhinged, his eyes wide and staring and his pale brown hair sticking up at the back.

'Please, Cody.' I glanced at my door. We were barely moving right now. Maybe I could try and leap out. I put my hand on the door handle.

'Stay *still*.' Cody's voice rose. His hand reached for the gun in his lap. 'Stay *still*, you bitch. You ratted me out, went to the police. You told them *everything*.'

'I *didn't*.' I bit my lip, my whole body trembling. 'I made one anonymous call. *Please*.'

The traffic ahead moved. Cody pressed on the accelerator and we sped away again. I looked around, but I couldn't see Flynn in any of the nearby cars. It was too much to hope he'd be able to follow Cody through all this traffic anyway. I slid my hand inside my jeans pocket. If I could get my phone out without Cody seeing, I could dial 999.

'*No!*' Cody raised his gun again. He glanced angrily across at me. 'Give me your mobile. And your bag.'

I handed everything over. My bag contained both my purse and Flynn's wallet. I felt lost without it.

'Where are we going?' I asked as we careered, too fast, around a bend in the road. 'You can't just—'

'Shut up,' Cody snapped. 'This is all your fault.'

'What?'

'You shouldn't have seen what you saw . . . Bentham giving me that cash, the order to . . . to . . . And you shouldn't have called the police.'

'Okay, but . . . but . . .' I hesitated, the enormity of my situation hitting me. It struck me that if I didn't go to the police now, I really was turning a blind eye to Cody and Bentham's horrific activities. Still, my first priority was to get away from Cody. I could still go to the cops even if I told Cody I wouldn't. 'You're not thinking straight,' I insisted. 'I just made one, anonymous call . . .' I caught my breath. 'Cody, I don't understand. This is all . . . totally outside anything I've ever done or seen or . . . or known. *Please*, I'm *terrified*.'

I turned, my eyes filling with tears, and stared out of the window. We were zooming past rows of terraced houses. They blurred in my vision. How could this be happening? I had never felt so sick with fear. Another minute passed. From the signs outside I could see we were heading north, towards the M1 motorway. As Cody turned on to another main road, he cleared his throat.

'You went to the police,' he said. 'I have a record already. It didn't take much to convince them I was guilty, even if they couldn't prove it. Plus Elmore – the guy I was supposed to "deal" with – has gone into hiding and Bentham is furious.'

'Okay, but . . . but that's over now,' I said. 'There's no point making things worse.'

Cody shook his head, muttering under his breath. We drove on, soon reaching the motorway. As we headed north a heavy rain started to fall from low, grey clouds. It struck me that I was nearly halfway to the commune. I badly wanted to be there again, among all the comforting and familiar sights and smells, with Dad and Gemma and Lily.

'How old are you?' I turned to Cody.

'Nineteen. Almost twenty,' he said. 'Why?'

I took a deep breath. 'You don't have to do any of this . . . work for Bentham . . . kidnap me . . . you've got *choices* . . .'

There was a long pause.

'I haven't kidnapped you,' Cody said.

'Okay, then . . . then stop the car and let me out.'

Cody swore but, to my surprise, he slowed the car.

144

'We'll stop and talk,' he snapped. 'That's all I'm promising.'

'Okay,' I said. 'Thank you.'

A moment later we pulled off the motorway and into a service station car park. It was still raining hard. Cody headed to the back of the car park, away from the other cars. As we drove past, a man got out of his mini. Pulling his hood up he hurried into the building with the shops and cafés. Apart from the few people who were huddled in the shelter of the entrance, puffing on cigarettes, there was no one else in sight.

Cody drove past all the parked cars, towards the trees that separated the shops and cafés from the petrol pumps. He pulled up, parking roughly beside a little corrugated iron shelter in a gap between the trees. As soon as he stopped, I grabbed the handle and pushed open my door.

'Come back!' Cody ordered. He lunged for me but I slid under his arm and out of the car. I charged across the tarmac. Cody reached me seconds later. He gripped my shoulder, swinging me around. The rain drummed down, cold on my shoulders.

'You stupid bitch,' he roared, raising his fist.

I flinched. But instead of hitting me, Cody yanked on my arm, pulling me backwards until we were under the corrugated iron shelter. Three large bins

145

overflowed with rubbish. Cody shoved me against the nearest bin and stood over me, panting heavily. His gun was in his fist, at his side.

I stood facing him, my heart thumping. All I could see was his face and the shelter wall beyond. All I could hear was his ragged breathing and the rain beating loudly on the iron roof. The stench of rotting meat filled my nostrils. I was totally hidden here from both the shopping area and the petrol pumps beyond. For a terrifying second I felt sure I was going to die, that – whatever Cody had said about talking – he had brought me here to kill me.

But Cody didn't move. He just stood over me, his whole body rigid with tension. I turned away, fear racing through my head. I couldn't think, couldn't focus. And then it suddenly struck me that maybe Cody was as terrified as I was, that he didn't really want to hurt me, that he simply didn't know whether he could trust me to keep quiet or not.

Which meant that all I needed to do was convince him and he would let me go.

I made myself look at him. 'Cody?' I said, keeping my voice as soft and steady as I could.

He glared at me.

'You said we could talk so . . . so tell me, what do I have to say to convince you that I'm not going to go back to the police?' In my heart I knew that as soon as I could, I was going to go straight to the nearest station, give my name and tell them exactly what I'd seen and heard. I had been wrong to keep quiet this long. Still, I didn't have to mean what I said to Cody. What counted was the here and now and getting away in one piece.

Cody shook his head. 'There isn't anything you can say.'

We stared at each other. I was struck, as I had been the first time I'd met him, by the coldness of his grey eyes. Flynn's eyes always burned with passion.

'Listen,' I said. 'If I was going to give a proper statement to the police with my name and everything, don't you think I'd have done it by now?'

Cody moved closer. I shrank back, past the bin, against the rough iron wall of the shelter. Cody placed one hand on the wall beside my head, then he lifted the gun out and pressed it against my side.

I wriggled sideways, trying to get away, but I was sandwiched between Cody and the huge metal bin. My heart was in my mouth.

'Please,' I begged. '*Please*, don't hurt me.'

There was a long, terrifying pause. Rain pounded against the shelter and then Cody leaned closer still.

'If I let you go and you tell *anyone* about what you saw, I will come after you, do you understand?'

I cowered at the low menace in his voice, my whole body shaking.

'Do you understand?' he repeated.

'Yes,' I gasped.

'If you breathe a word, I will hunt you down. You *and* Flynn. I will kill you *both*.'

'You all right, love?' A male voice cut in over Cody's threatening whisper.

Cody spun around, pushing me in front of him, concealing his gun between us. I could feel the metal barrel pressing against my back.

The man who had interrupted us was standing just outside the shelter. He wore a yellow uniform, a bin bag in his hand. His eyes widened as he saw the look of terror on my face. He dropped the bag. It landed with a thud on the ground.

'What's going on?' he said. 'Do you know this guy? Are you okay?'

'She's fine.' Cody pressed the gun more firmly against my back. 'Tell him.'

'I . . . I . . .' I could barely speak, I was so scared. I felt a strong urge to pee.

Then the man strode right up to us. 'She's obviously not fine,' he said angrily. 'Come with me, love.'

He reached for my arm. Cody pushed him. And then everything seemed to happen at once. Cody and the man struggled for a second. They spun around, staggering across the shelter, then outside into the rain. I caught a flash of Cody's gun, glinting wet. And then a shot fired.

I gasped. Cody backed away from the man, who slumped to the ground, his eyes closed. I stared at him, time slowing down. Blood was seeping across his yellow uniform. He lay still. Rain drummed on the shelter. In the distance I could hear raised voices, people shouting out, asking where the shot had come from.

I stared down at the man. Someone ran over. Shook my arm.

'River? Are you all right?' It was Flynn.

Relief flooded through me at the sound of his voice. I turned to face him. His eyes were wide, full of fear for me. I blinked, unable to speak.

'Did he hurt you?' Flynn asked.

I shook my head. The man on the ground still hadn't moved. Cody was standing, wide-eyed, just a metre away, the gun still in his hand. Flynn darted over to the man. He dropped to the ground and pressed his fingers against the man's neck. Time seemed to stop altogether and then Flynn looked up. His face was drained of colour. He turned to Cody.

'He's dead,' he said. 'You killed him.'

15

I tore my eyes away from the body on the ground. Cody was standing, open-mouthed, the gun still in his hand. Flynn stood up. He backed away from Cody and reached out for me.

'Okay, Cody,' he said. 'River and I are going to leave now.'

I took Flynn's hand. He held it tightly, pulling me towards him. I stumbled across the rough concrete. Litter fluttered around my feet – a burger wrapper, an old scrap of newspaper. My brain couldn't seem to process what had just happened. I looked back at the man on the ground. His face was still, his eyes closed. He looked asleep. Yet blood seeped from his stomach. He was dead, Flynn had said.

Dead.

I couldn't take it in. A whole life wiped out. Someone's husband. Someone's son.

Flynn kept his eyes on Cody as we backed away,

past the shelter, towards the car park. The rain had slowed to a drizzle, a light mist on my face. I held tightly to Flynn's hand.

'I didn't mean this to happen,' Cody said. His eyes were blank with shock. 'It was an accident, I was just trying to push him away.'

'We know,' Flynn said soothingly. 'We know, it's okay.'

I glanced around as we edged further backwards. In the distance I could see people running around, clearly still trying to work out where the gunshot had come from.

'Stop!' Cody said.

I looked back at him. He had raised his gun again. His hand shook as he cocked the weapon. 'I can't let you leave,' he insisted.

Flynn gently drew me behind him so that he stood between me and Cody. 'You don't have a choice,' he said, keeping his voice soft and low. 'River and I have done nothing wrong. You can't keep us or—'

'I can do what I like,' Cody snapped, a cold arrogance returning to his voice. 'Get in the car.'

'No. Cody, this isn't like when Bentham orders a hit,' Flynn insisted. 'River and I can both see that what happened was an accident. But it still happened. And if you hurt us you'll just make things

151

worse. You *have* to let us go.' As Flynn spoke those last words an edge of panic crept into his voice.

'I'll explain what happened,' I added. 'The guy was trying to stop you hassling me. There was a fight. I'll tell everyone you didn't shoot him on purpose.'

Cody marched towards us. Flynn stiffened, his arm reaching around, checking I was still safe behind him. I moved away, facing Cody down.

'*Please*, Cody,' I said, staring at the gun in Cody's hand.

'Get in my car.' Cody pressed the gun against my ribs so hard that I gasped. He glanced at Flynn. 'Both of you.'

'All right. Okay, just don't hurt her.' Flynn held up his hands in surrender but I could see the fury – and the fear – burning in his eyes. He backed away as Cody shoved me towards his car.

'Get in the back,' Cody ordered. I fumbled with the door handle, my hands shaking.

Cody turned to Flynn. 'You can drive,' he said.

We all got in the car. Flynn's jaw was clenched as he took the keys from Cody and started the engine.

'Go.' Cody levelled his gun at Flynn's chest.

Flynn put the car in reverse. As we pulled on to the main part of the concourse, two men ran towards us. One was pointing beyond us, towards the body of the man on the floor. The other turned and looked, horrified, into the car. I couldn't tell if he saw Cody's gun, but he must have sensed we were somehow involved with the shooting because he waved his arms.

'Hey!' he shouted, trying to flag us down.

'Go!' Cody insisted. He thrust his gun at Flynn's ribs.

Flynn stepped on the accelerator and we roared away. I looked around, through the back window. I half expected someone to be following us, but the two men were now bending over the dead man's body and no other vehicles were moving through the service station.

We turned on to the M1. Flynn drove north at Cody's instruction. The rain stopped and the sun came out. None of us spoke. The shock of what had just happened settled inside me.

Cody had killed someone. I had witnessed the murder.

It changed everything.

After a while, Cody demanded to know how Flynn had found us and Flynn explained that he'd followed us in his car, not realising we'd left the motorway until after the turning, then doubling back.

'I heard the shot just after I saw your car,' Flynn

said. 'I was only a few metres away, on the other side of those bins.'

I cleared my throat. My whole body felt tight and tense. 'Cody, please, where are you taking us?'

Cody ignored me.

'Do you even have a plan?' I went on. 'I saw you kill that man. We can tell everyone that it was an accident, but you have to take responsibility for what you did, you have—'

'I don't *have* to do anything.' Cody swore. He kept his gun trained on Flynn, but glanced over his shoulder at where I was sitting on the back seat. 'Nobody knows we were even at that service station. No one saw us.'

'At least two people saw this car,' Flynn pointed out. 'And the three of us inside it.'

'We're going to dump the car soon.' Cody pressed the gun against Flynn's ribs, making me gasp. 'Take the next turning.'

I sat back, my heart racing. Flynn drove on in silence. After a minute or so, Cody took the gun away from his side and laid it in his lap. None of us spoke as Flynn pulled off the motorway.

I glanced at the road signs but couldn't seem to take in the names. I'd never heard of any of the places. Cody ordered Flynn to take a series of turnings, gradually steering him away from the main roads.

We drove on for another thirty minutes. It was late afternoon now. Mum would be wondering where I was, maybe even making phone calls to my friends. Dad would most likely be on his way back from the commune with Stone. He had probably texted me already to tell me when he would arrive at Mum's and that he wanted to pick me up straight away so that he could hurry home to Gemma and Lily.

I felt a pang of misery and guilt at the worry my silence would cause them all. They didn't deserve any more anxiety because of me. I looked at Flynn, still driving. His jaw was clenched, his shoulders hunched. He was angry and scared, and trying not to show he was frightened. I thought of the way he had stood between Cody and me when Cody raised his gun.

That was love, wasn't it? True love? I closed my eyes. I couldn't seem to think straight about anything. All around me was chaos. Ahead only danger.

'I need to let my parents know I'm okay,' I said at last. 'Seriously, they'll—'

'Shut up,' Cody snapped.

Flynn glanced at him. I could see he was itching to tell him not to talk to me like that, but fearful that antagonising Cody might provoke him to start waving his gun about again.

155

We were travelling along a small country lane now. I had no idea exactly where we were. Cody seemed to know the area well, giving Flynn precise instructions about which turnings to take. We drove and drove. The sun grew lower in the sky. And still we drove. I was desperately thirsty, though too scared to feel remotely hungry, and I badly needed to pee.

At last Cody told Flynn to stop the car close to some trees. He got Flynn out and forced him on to his knees on the ground, then ordered me outside too.

'I need to go to the loo,' I said.

'In the trees,' Cody said.

He let me go over behind the nearest tree. Despite the earlier rain it was a mild evening, only a soft breeze cooling the warm air. As I peed on to the ground, I thought about making a dash for it. Cody wasn't far away, of course, but maybe I could lose him in the wood.

What about Flynn? I couldn't leave him here.

I stood up, a new determination filling me. There were two of us against only one Cody. I was quick and Flynn was both quick and strong. Surely, between us, we could overpower him, gun or no gun?

I strode back to the two of them. Flynn was still

kneeling on the ground, his hands clasped behind his head.

'Get up,' Cody demanded.

As Flynn got to his feet, I caught his eye, trying to signal my intention that I was ready to fight and to run. He gave me a quick, sharp nod. We walked through the trees single file: me first, then Flynn, with Cody just behind him. I could hardly breathe, waiting for Flynn's signal. He was still trying to talk to Cody, to calm him down, but I could hear in his voice that he held out little hope of being able to reason with him. Neither did I. Cody seemed totally in control of himself, showing no sign of his earlier panic. I didn't know where he was taking us or what he was going to do, but it was obvious he had some definite plan in mind.

'There's no way out of this, wherever we hide,' Flynn was saying. 'You have to sleep, you'll have to find food and water, you'll be on the run *and* you'll have us to deal with. It's too much.'

Cody said nothing. He was keeping his gun firmly trained on Flynn, only occasionally glancing over at me.

'The police will find your car, even if you dump it,' I added. 'They'll work out where we are.'

'I'll get another car,' Cody said, suddenly breaking his silence. His voice was like a chip of ice. 'I'll burn the old one, it'll take ages for the police to connect it with me.'

We reached the edge of the trees and emerged on to an open field. The ground was rough and strewn with pebbles across the grass. Cody forced us on. I stumbled over the stones and Flynn reached out his hand to steady me.

'Get back!' Cody ordered.

Flynn let his hand fall to his side.

We walked on. The ground sloped sharply upwards as we rounded the corner of the field. I gasped. We were higher up than I'd realised. A white chasm opened up in front of us. Chains with *Keep Out* notices ran along the edge.

'Where are we?' I asked.

Cody said nothing.

'It's a chalk quarry,' Flynn said.

I stared down at the ravine, its white walls roughly hewn out of the earth.

'Why are we here?' Fear gripped my throat.

Cody ordered us under the chain. We shuffled forwards to the very edge of the quarry.

'On your knees, both of you,' he ordered. 'Hands behind your head.'

I sank to the ground. Flynn knelt beside me. Cody levelled his gun at the back of Flynn's head and I suddenly realised what he was about to do.

'*No.*' The word slipped out of me, a desperate gasp.

'I don't have a choice.' Cody cocked his revolver.

The world spun around me. He was going to shoot Flynn. Then me. Our bodies would fall into the quarry. Our lives would end. I couldn't take it in and yet it was happening.

Right here.

Right now.

I glanced at Flynn. He was already looking at me and the focused fury in his eyes gave me strength. He hadn't given up. I shouldn't either.

I looked over at Cody. His arm was outstretched, the gun pressed against the back of Flynn's head. His hand was shaking. There was terror in his eyes but he was psyching himself up to shoot.

Flynn was still looking at me. His body was tensed, poised, ready for a chance to fight.

I had to do something. *Now.* Everything depended on it.

I took a deep breath and stood up.

16

I backed away from the edge. Cody swung his gun arm around, so the weapon pointed at me.

'What are you doing?' he yelled. 'Get dow—!'

With a roar, Flynn hurled himself at Cody's legs. Cody fell to the ground with a thud. Flynn pressed him back, trying to force the gun out of Cody's hand. For a second it wavered dangerously in Flynn's face, then, with another yell, Flynn punched at Cody's arm.

The gun sailed out of his hand and into the quarry below. Cody was trying to push Flynn away, but Flynn was punching him, all flying fists. He rammed into Cody's face, pummelling as hard as he could. One. Two. Three blows. Cody lay, dazed and blinking, on the ground. Flynn sat back, fist raised, ready to strike again. For once I felt myself *wanting* him to land another punch, to knock Cody out properly. He deserved it.

As soon as I'd thought this, I was filled with a terrible fear that Flynn would seriously hurt Cody and that, despite what Cody had done, this would be wrong.

'That's enough.' I crept over to Flynn.

He nodded, his breath heavy and jagged. 'Where's the gun?' he asked.

I pointed over the ravine. 'Down there,' I said.

'Good.' Flynn stood up. 'Let's go.'

I stared down at Cody. He was groaning now, his hand feeling his jaw. 'We can't just leave him here,' I said.

'We can't stay, either.' Flynn took my arm and started running. 'Come on. We have to get away.'

He was right. I let him lead me around the edge of the chalk quarry and across to the other side. As we reached the edge of the trees opposite, we stopped for a second to catch our breath. I looked back. Cody was struggling to his feet. He looked around, but clearly couldn't see us all the way over here by the trees. He started walking slowly away from the ravine edge. Even from this distance it was obvious he was still dazed.

'He's heading back to his car,' Flynn said quietly beside me. 'He thinks we'll have tried to steal it, drive off somewhere.'

'Where are we going to go?' I asked, the enormity

161

of the situation weighing down on top of me. 'I saw Cody kill someone, I have to tell the police.'

Flynn said nothing. A deep frown creased his forehead.

'What?' I said.

'I . . . you're right about going to the police. It's just . . . it's like before . . . I'm worried that if you give a statement about Cody, it will bring Bentham into the whole thing . . .'

'Why?'

'If you tell the police you saw Cody kill that man, you'll have to explain why you were with him in the first place . . . which means saying what you saw back at the Blue Parrot . . . which implicates Bentham.'

'But Bentham wasn't anywhere near that motorway car park.'

'I know, but he's linked to Cody.' Flynn sighed. 'Listen, Lance Bentham makes Cody Walsh look like a saint. If he thinks you or Cody might implicate him in any way, he'll do *anything* to shut you up. I . . . I know he will . . . It's happened with other witnesses.' Flynn looked at me. 'Bentham has friends in the police anyway. I'm not even sure they'll follow through on what you tell them.'

'But why would Bentham care?' I asked. 'I didn't even see his face when I was at the Blue Parrot, I couldn't identify him from a line-up. I only saw *Cody* properly. That's not enough proof against Bentham – why should he worry?'

'Because of all that happened in Bentham's bar, because Cody works for him, because the link between them is too strong.' Flynn sighed. 'Even if your evidence can't hurt Bentham directly, it helps the police get closer to prosecuting him. Either way, you'll be in terrible danger, Riv.' He paused. 'I've *put* you in terrible danger by getting involved with Bentham in the first place.'

I looked down. Everything Flynn said was true, including that last part. He might not have meant his choices to threaten my life, but they had.

'You're right, Flynn,' I said. 'You have to take some of the responsibility for me meeting Cody and for putting me in this position, but a man is still dead and I saw it happen and I can't let Cody get away with that. So *I* have to take responsibility for what I witnessed which means I have to tell the police – it's just the right thing to do.'

There was a long pause. 'Okay,' Flynn finally conceded.

I reached into my pocket, but Cody had taken my phone. I made a face. 'Can I borrow your mobile? I need to call Dad as well as the cops.'

Flynn handed me his phone, but there was no

signal, so we walked on in silence through the wood. I had no idea where we were, or where we were heading. After about twenty minutes, a breeze whipped up, cooling the air. I shivered and Flynn took his jacket and put it over my shoulders. We carried on walking, the snap of twigs and crunch of the dry earth underfoot the only sound all around us. After a while, Flynn cleared his throat.

'Do you still have my wallet?' he asked.

'No, Cody took it in the car along with my phone and my purse.' I made a face. 'The only thing in my pocket is the iPod you gave me.'

'So you've got no money at all?'

'What about you?'

Flynn shook his head. 'I gave you almost everything I had. I've been living off the rest since last week. I'm down to my last few quid.'

'It won't matter,' I said. 'We've still got your phone. As soon as we've got a signal we can call for help. If the police won't pick us up I'm sure my dad will.'

Flynn took a deep breath.

'Riv, I know you're right about talking to the police but I've been thinking and I want you to let *me* do it. I'm in bad with Bentham anyway. I can tell the police everything they need to know about Cody killing that guy, make out I was there, not you, then you won't have to—'

'Weren't you listening to what I said earlier?' I interrupted. 'I was right there. You didn't even *see* the shooting. It's wrong not to—'

'But it's the only way to keep Bentham away from you and still do the right thing.'

I stopped walking. We were near the edge of the trees now, the lights of a row of buildings clearly visible beyond the wood.

'No, Flynn,' I said firmly. 'I know you want to protect me, but I have to take responsibility for what I saw. Don't pressure me to do something different. This is who I am. It's important. You have to let me be me, not try and turn me into a scaredy-cat victim because *you're* scared I might get hurt.'

Flynn opened his mouth to protest, then closed it again. He smiled.

'You've changed,' he said.

'I've just been alone a lot,' I said. 'I'm used to making my own decisions now.'

'Okay,' he said. 'You're right. We'll *both* go to the police. We'll *both* tell the truth.'

It was dark when we emerged from the trees to find ourselves in a residential street. The houses opposite were large and detached. A sign at the crossroads nearby pointed to the town centre. I checked Flynn's phone. At last there was a signal.

'I need to make the call,' I said.

Flynn nodded. 'Whatever you want to do, I'm in.'

I hesitated, staring up at the town centre sign. Once we had talked to the police, Mum and Dad would almost certainly come and take me away. After that, it would be hard to see Flynn, certainly for a while. If he admitted his involvement with Bentham, he might well be arrested and charged, and I could just imagine how Mum and Dad would react to that. In the end, none of the detail of what we had said and done would count for anything. All Mum and Dad would see was that Flynn was back and I was mixed up in a whole lot of danger and trouble.

I pressed 999 and lifted the phone to my ear. The operator answered straight away, asking which service I needed.

'Police,' I said. 'There was ... an incident at a service station. I don't know which one but it was off the M1, not far outside London. I saw a man in a yellow uniform get shot. He was killed. Then the man who did it, Cody Walsh, he kidnapped me and my friend. He tried to kill us too.'

The operator started speaking again, but I wasn't listening to her. I was staring at Flynn. There was such misery in his eyes. I knew he was thinking the same as I had been, that after this it would be hard to see each other, that everyone we knew would want to keep us apart, that this precious time together would be over.

'I'm not able to say any more right now,' I said into the phone, cutting over the operator who was still speaking. I looked at Flynn. He raised his eyebrows. 'I've told you what happened. I promise I'll come into a station and give a statement tomorrow morning.'

Flynn's eyes widened as I turned off the call.

'What was that?' he said.

I moved closer, putting my hands on his shoulders. 'I just thought . . .' I said, '. . . that it's already late and there isn't anything more I can tell the police that will make a difference right now, so we might as well have tonight together, then go to the police in the morning. I'll say what I saw at the Blue Parrot and at the service station, and you can explain about Bentham and . . . and hopefully they'll protect us.'

A huge grin spread over Flynn's face. He wrapped his arms around my waist and pulled me towards him. 'Spend the night together?' he said. 'Are you sure?'

I nodded. 'We can sleep rough, it's not *that* cold.'

Flynn looked sceptical. 'It'll get a lot colder overnight, but yes, definitely, yes.' He bent his head and kissed me, soft, on the lips.

A delicious thrill threaded through me. I smiled. 'So much for getting to know each other slowly again.'

'Well things will certainly get slower once your parents hear I'm back.' Flynn sighed. 'They'll be mad that you're seeing me.'

'I know.' I leaned against him, running my hands over the back of his jacket, feeling the strong muscles underneath. 'Maybe we should just run away together.'

'Mmm.' Flynn hugged me tighter. 'Running away might *sound* romantic but I've done it before, without you, and it sucks and it's not the right thing, either. You shouldn't be away from your parents and your friends and college and your whole life.'

'Okay, then, we sleep rough tonight and go to the police tomorrow, like I just promised them.' I kissed him again. Then we took each other's hand and crossed the road. As we followed the sign to the town centre, anxiety swirled in my stomach. The plan we'd made to tell the police everything was definitely the right course of action. And yet it was going to be so hard. I glanced at Flynn, loving the feel of his strong fingers clasping mine. At least I had him.

It was ironic how Flynn had brought such chaos into my life and yet, even after everything that had happened, being with him still felt so right. What was it he'd said?

You're the only person I'll ever truly love. That's what's in the stars, not what all those other people think.

We reached the end of one road and turned on to a busier, shopping street. The wind was cooler now. I tugged Flynn's jacket around me. 'I should call home, just to say I'm okay, then we can switch the mobile off.'

Flynn pointed to a pub. 'I'm going in there. I've got a good idea for getting some money so maybe we won't have to sleep outside after all.'

'Okay.' I wasn't really paying attention. I stood on the pavement, his phone in my hand. What was I going to say to Mum and Dad? Then it struck me. I had no idea what their mobile numbers were. The data was stored in my phone which was still with Cody. It was the same with my friends' mobile numbers. And I didn't know the landline number for the commune either. In fact, the only telephone number I could remember was the one from Mum's house which she'd drilled into me many years ago, when I was at primary school, before I had my own mobile phone.

I hesitated. A car drove past at high speed. I didn't really have a choice. I had to let my parents know I was okay. I had been gone now for hours. Reluctantly

I pressed the digits on the phone pad. Mum answered after just one ring.

'Hello?' I could hear her desperation in that single word. Guilt pulsed through me.

'Mum?'

'Oh, River.' Mum sucked in her breath. 'Where are you? Are you all right?'

'I'm fine, Mum. I . . .' I stopped, unsure how to explain what had happened to me today without scaring her to death.

'I've been so worried,' Mum went on. 'I called Grace and Leo and they had no idea where you were. I really want you home now. Your dad's here. He's been trying you too, he was planning on heading back to the commune hours ago.'

'I know,' I said. 'Please tell him I'm sorry.'

'Tell him yourself,' Mum said. 'But first tell me when you'll be back. Where are you? Did you just lose track of time?'

'Er, yeah, that's right . . .' I tailed off again.

'River, what's wrong?' Mum drew in her breath sharply. 'Is this something to do with Flynn?'

His name hung in the air between us.

I hesitated. 'I'm fine, Mum. I'm really sorry, but some stuff happened earlier, stuff I . . . I need to sort out. I have to go, but I'll be home tomorrow.' I rang off.

A few seconds later the phone rang. Mum's home number flashed on the screen. I turned off the call. A minute later and the phone rang a second time, this time showing what I was sure was Mum's mobile. Or maybe Dad's. I closed my eyes. I should have blocked the number before making the call.

I switched off the whole phone and shoved it into Flynn's jacket pocket.

I was about to head into the pub when Flynn himself emerged. I opened my mouth to tell him about my conversation with Mum, then realised he wasn't alone. Three men and a girl were following him out of the pub. They looked like they were in their late teens too, all of them laughing and shouting in the night air.

Flynn caught my eye. 'I've got a way of getting us some money, Riv,' he said quietly. 'It should be enough to pay for a proper hotel . . .' He took my hand, letting the others pass then following them along the pavement. 'A proper last night before we have to go back to hardly seeing each other.'

I frowned. 'How will those people help us get money?' I whispered.

'It's a bet,' Flynn said. 'I've bet them two hundred pounds I can beat them at bronco.'

I stared at him. 'What's bronco?' I asked.

Flynn grinned. 'It's a game I used to play when I

first met Cody. It's stupid but there's a knack to it and I'm good. I *know* I can win.'

The group had reached a car. Two of the men got inside the front. One indicated the back seat for me and Flynn.

Flynn moved to open the door but I held him back. 'What will you have to do in this game?' I hissed.

Ahead of us, the remaining guy and the girl were getting into the Volvo parked just in front. Flynn tugged at my hand. 'Come on, Riv, it's just a thing with cars.'

'Cars?' I said, as he opened the rear door. 'You mean like a racing game?'

'Not exactly,' Flynn said. 'But it *is* a competition. Anyway, it's a lot easier than it looks so you mustn't worry. I'll be fine.' This was hardly reassuring, but the engine was already running, so I followed Flynn into the car.

As we drove off, the guy in the passenger seat up front turned and smiled. 'I'm Josh,' he said.

'River,' I said. This was getting surreal though Josh seemed friendly enough. 'Er, where are we going?'

'Ex-factory car park,' Josh said. He glanced at Flynn. 'There should be enough space there, yeah?'

'From what Gazza said in the pub it sounds perfect,' Flynn said with a nod.

I leaned over, whispering in his ear. 'Perfect for *what*, though?'

'Bronco,' he said. 'Don't worry, Riv. I've told you, it's cool. We'll be done in under an hour, then we can find somewhere to stay.' He smiled and squeezed my hand.

I sat back. Flynn could smile all he liked, but nothing he was saying was reassuring me. A game called bronco involving cars and strangers sounded almost as dangerous as what we'd already been through tonight with Cody.

17

We drove for about fifteen minutes, quickly leaving behind the small town. Flynn seemed amazingly relaxed, chatting away to the two guys up front like he'd known them for weeks already. Their names were Josh and Jonny and most of their conversation revolved around how 'mad' their mate Gazza – in the car in front – was . . . and how Flynn would never beat him at bronco.

I still had no idea how this game involving cars worked, but it sounded highly risky. Taking risks, apparently, was Gazza's 'thing'.

'He loves pushing it to the edge,' Josh said with relish.

'Yeah, he's *crazy*,' Jonny added. 'Total adrenalin junkie.'

I rolled my eyes. Why did some boys get so excited about what seemed to me fundamentally stupid behaviour?

A few minutes later we pulled up in a large car park which, as the boys had explained, was out the back of an old factory. The building was clearly unused and verging on the derelict. *Keep Out* notices were dotted everywhere. They reminded me of the notices at the top of the chalk quarry. It seemed impossible that Cody had held a gun to our heads just a few hours ago. Everything that had happened earlier today felt like a bad dream.

'Okay so which car do we use?' Josh asked, as Gazza emerged from the Volvo.

I glanced at his girlfriend. She was pretty, with short blonde hair and big earrings, but she looked bored. Well, that was something. Perhaps whatever Flynn and Gazza were about to do wouldn't be all that dangerous after all.

The four guys stood in a huddle, sorting out the rules and arguing over who was going to drive the car in the contest. I smiled at Gazza's girlfriend.

'Hi, I'm River,' I said.

'Sal,' she said with a quick smile back.

I wanted to ask her if she knew about the game the boys were about to play, but before I could say anything Flynn was by my side, drawing me away.

'Okay, Riv,' he whispered. 'We're about to start, wish me luck.'

'I still don't understand what you're going to do,' I said. 'Are you sure you won't get hurt?'

'I won't.' Flynn grinned. 'I told you, I've done this before. With Cody and some of the other Bentham guys.'

I shook my head. This felt so surreal.

'Come on then.' Gazza swaggered over. He was big, well over six feet, with a scar across his forehead and cropped hair. I hoped that whatever bronco was about it didn't involve a fist fight. Gazza's girlfriend seemed to shrink back into the shadows as Gazza loomed over us. He didn't look at her. I took an instant dislike to him.

'I'm ready,' Flynn said calmly.

Heart in my mouth, I watched as Jonny drove him and Gazza to the centre of the car park. They stopped about thirty metres from where Josh, Sal and I were standing.

'What happens now?' Sal asked. She sounded as nervous as I felt.

'I'm not sure,' I said. 'Don't you know this game either?'

'No,' Sal said, fidgeting from foot to foot. 'It's your boyfriend's idea. Gazza's well excited about it.'

'It sounds ace,' Josh butted in. 'Gazza'll be brilliant at it.'

My heart drummed against my ribs as Flynn and

Gazza got out of the car, then clambered on to the roof. Jonny stayed in the driver's seat, revving the engine. I noticed all four windows were open.

'What are they doing?' My throat was dry.

Sal's hand was over her mouth. Josh grinned.

Flynn and Gazza lay across the top of the car next to each other. They gripped the underside of the roof on the gap made by the wound-down windows. Flynn tucked his feet under the roof on the other side. Gazza immediately did the same. If Jonny, still inside, chose to wind up the windows, their toes and hands would have been trapped. But Jonny just revved the engine. Clearly this was all part of the game.

'Ready?' Jonny shouted.

'Yes.' Flynn and Gazza spoke at once. They both sounded tense and determined.

A second later the car raced away.

'D'you get it now, Sal?' Josh asked. 'It's bucking bronco, but with a car instead of a horse.'

I stared at the two boys as the car screeched across the empty car park. I couldn't believe it. The game that Flynn was playing for two hundred pounds was *recklessly* dangerous.

'Are you saying that they have to stay on the roof?' I breathed. 'While the driver swerves around and tries to throw them off?'

'Exactly,' Josh said with a chuckle.

'Oh my days,' Sal gasped.

I watched, my stomach churning over and over. Jonny, having started in a straight line, was now reversing. Flynn and Gazza had their heads down. Even from here I could see how hard they were both working to keep their bodies flat against the roof of the car.

Jonny moved the car forwards again, this time zigzagging at top speed across the tarmac. I glanced at the ground. If Flynn got thrown off the car he could break a leg or an arm landing . . . maybe even his neck.

'Oh God, oh God.' My eyes felt like they were on stalks as I willed him to stay on.

'Come on, Gazza!' Josh shouted out beside me.

The car was going faster and faster, the two boys on its roof a dizzying blur. Gazza's legs splayed out behind him, his feet sticking out from the top of the car. My throat felt swollen as I prayed for Flynn to stay on, to be safe.

A huge roar filled the air. I couldn't work out whether it was Jonny or Flynn or Gazza calling out. Only about twenty seconds had passed, but it felt like an eternity. The car swerved and spun, going faster and faster. An arm flew out. Was that Flynn or Gazza? It took a second for me to process it was Flynn. He was surely about to fly into the air, to crash to the ground.

18

I gasped as Flynn gripped the side of the car again. His head was down, his whole body tensed. Another roar and Gazza's legs slid down, over the back windscreen. The car spun. Seconds fired away. Flynn was still on the roof but Gazza was half off the car, his hands losing their grip.

With a final yell, Gazza flew off the roof of the car. He landed on his side, metres away on the tarmac. A few moments later the car braked. Flynn lay on the roof, panting, then swung himself off on to the ground on the opposite side of the car. He staggered sideways a few steps, dropping to his knees. I broke into a run, racing over towards him. I was dimly aware of Sal and Josh running too, heading for Gazza, but all I could see was Flynn.

He was still kneeling when I reached him. I crouched down. His eyes were tight shut, his face pale.

'Flynn?' I leaned in close. 'Flynn, are you all right?'

He opened his eyes. Colour was already coming back to his cheeks.

'Fine,' he panted. 'Just a bit dizzy.'

I straightened up, my relief turning to fierce, hot anger. Flynn felt across the ground, then pushed himself to his feet. He glanced towards the spot a few metres away where Gazza was struggling to stand up, surrounded by his friends.

Flynn turned to me and grinned. 'Hey, I won, Riv. That means we've got enough money to sleep somewhere really nice.'

I shook my head, now so furious I couldn't even speak.

Flynn frowned. 'What is it?' he said. 'You look mad. But I won. I'm fine. We'll get the two hundred quid. I—'

'You could have *died*,' I blurted out. As I spoke, tears sprang to my eyes. 'You took a stupid risk just to get us a *bed*. Don't you get it, Flynn? We saw someone *die* earlier. And here you are acting like an idiot just so we don't have to spend one night outside.'

'So *you* wouldn't have to.' Flynn now looked bewildered. 'I did bronco for *you*, Riv. I thought you'd—'

'Don't you dare make it all about me,' I said. 'I didn't *ask* you to risk your neck like that. I don't care where we sleep. I just wanted to have some time with you before we have to face the police and my parents and everything goes horrible again.' Tears choked my throat. Flynn reached out, his forehead creased with concern. Infuriated I pushed his hand away. 'Don't.'

We looked at each other.

'Are you saying you don't want me to stay? That you just want to go to the police?' Flynn asked, his voice hollow.

I hesitated. The truth was, I didn't know what I wanted. My whole life felt like it had been turned upside down in the past few hours. And then, out of the corner of my eye, I saw Gazza and Sal getting into the car in the middle of the car park. Jonny was already inside, Josh pelting back towards the second car.

I gasped. They were running away.

'Hey!' I shouted. 'Come back.'

Flynn spun around. 'Oy, you owe me!' he yelled.

We raced towards the nearest car, but Jonny was already revving the engine. Seconds later it zoomed off. Flynn chased after Josh, but he was metres ahead. Another few moments and he, also, was inside his car and roaring away.

Flynn stopped running. I reached him. We stood, catching our breath.

'Great,' Flynn said bitterly. 'All that effort and we don't have our money *and* you're mad at me.'

For some reason, the way he said it made me laugh. It just all felt so crazy, like we were living in some surreal dream. My laugh grew into a guffaw. I bent over, knowing that I was being hysterical but unable to stop.

Flynn watched me laugh, then a smile spread over his face too and, soon, we were laughing together. I reached out and held Flynn in my arms. Seconds later we were kissing.

Flynn pulled away. 'So you're *not* mad?' he asked, raising his eyebrows.

'Of course I'm mad,' I said with a sigh. 'Playing that stupid game was crazy. And pointless, as it turned out. But it doesn't mean I don't want to be with you.'

Flynn put his arm around my shoulders. 'Okay, so we've confirmed two things: that I'm an idiot and that you love me anyway. Right?'

I laughed again. 'Right.'

He squeezed my shoulder. 'Then I guess we're back on track.'

'Except we have no idea where we are,' I said.

'Actually I *do* know,' Flynn said with a cocky grin. 'There's a town called Starhaven about six miles away by road.'

I made a face. 'Six miles?' It was already late and the wind was picking up. Now that this afternoon's trauma and the recent terror of the bronco game were over, I felt exhausted.

'What's the point in walking for six miles,' I said with a yawn. I pointed to the abandoned factory on the far side of the car park. 'We might as well just spend the night in there.'

Flynn made a face. 'We can do better than that. Anyway, we *don't* have to walk six miles. When I was talking to those guys in the pub they said this factory was just half a mile from the sea.'

'So?' I pulled my hood up, over my head, shielding my ears from the wind. Now Flynn mentioned it, I could smell the tang of ozone in that sharp wind.

'So . . . there's some coastal path that cuts the journey by miles. If we get a move on, we can be in a proper town with hotels in about an hour.'

Flynn reached for my hand, but instead of letting him take it, I shrugged. 'What's the point of walking *anywhere*, we still won't have any money when we get there?'

A slow, sexy smile spread over Flynn's face. 'Won't we?' He opened the hand he had held out to me. I gasped. There, on his palm, were two scrunched-up twenty-pound notes.

'Where did you get them?' I asked.

'They were poking out of Gazza's pocket when we got on the car,' Flynn said. He affected a modest smile. 'I thought I'd better take them for safekeeping, in case they fell out.'

'Yeah, right.' I raised my eyebrows. 'You were that sure you'd win, were you?'

'I told you I would. Bronco's an insane game, unless you know the knack of it. Which I do.' Flynn chuckled as he shoved the money in his pocket. 'Come on, let's find the sea.'

I took his hand and we walked away from the factory and towards the road. It was deserted. We hurried along the kerbside until we came to a sign showing the coastal path Flynn said we needed to take. It was almost 10.30 p.m. now and the way was dark, firstly across fields then through a wood. The air grew chillier as we walked. Soon the fresh salt tang of the sea grew stronger. Another few metres and we could hear the roar of the waves.

We emerged from the trees on to a pathway that sloped gently down the cliff towards the beach below. 'Look.' Flynn pointed across the dark expanse of water that stretched away from us, to the brightly lit town across the bay.

'That's where we're headed,' he said. 'Starhaven.'

We walked on, side by side along the path, our arms now around each other's backs. It felt so natural to be holding each other like this and – for a while – our conversation flowed naturally too. I told Flynn about sixth form and making friends with Emmi again. He told me more about his life since he left the commune, how he'd rented his flat using pay from being Bentham's bodyguard, how shocked he'd felt when he discovered just how brutal Bentham really was.

'I didn't really think about how immoral it was at first, hiding guns for Bentham,' Flynn said, his voice full of self-loathing. 'I only thought about helping Mum and . . . and that it would be hard to say "no" to my boss, that I'd probably lose my bodyguard job if I did.' He hesitated.

'And that your job paid a lot of money, which you didn't want to give up?' I asked, drily.

Flynn nodded, a miserable shadow haunting his face. 'It was just so brilliant being able to have what I wanted: my own flat and the car . . . nice clothes. But none of it made me happy. I'd thought for so long that having money would make everything else all right, but it doesn't, Riv. It just means you can buy nice stuff to distract you from how miserable you really are.'

We walked on in silence, lost in our own thoughts. Flynn seemed like a different person from the boy I'd met nearly two years ago, all mouth and swagger, certain he knew the answers to everything. He was still confident – and liable to do reckless things, as that game of bronco had proved – but there was a new humility about him too, an honesty and an acceptance that he had got things wrong in the past. It made him seem more open . . . stronger somehow.

And even more lovable.

It began to rain again as we strolled down the cliff, just a light patter on our shoulders, but enough to speed us up. The path narrowed and grew steeper as we descended. Beneath us the tide was out, revealing stretches of stony beach. I crept a little closer to the edge of the path, peering down at the sea many metres below.

'There are lots of little bays down here,' I said. 'Do you think there are caves in the rock face?'

'Come back from the edge.' Flynn's voice was suddenly harsh.

I took a step back, irritated. Flynn might be more humble than he used to be, but he still had a tendency to be overbearing. 'I wasn't anywhere *near* the edge.'

'It's dangerous. Cliff paths can crumble easily, especially when it's wet,' Flynn said stubbornly.

'You've got a nerve,' I snapped, turning to face him. 'Lecturing *me* on what's freaking dangerous.

You worked for a gangster. You made friends with someone who has *killed* people for that gangster. You brought him to your sister's wedding for goodness sake.'

'I didn't have anyone else I could ask,' Flynn said. 'None of my old friends would have come with me, and—'

'Well whose fault is *that*?' I said, the rain wet on my face. 'You make it impossible for people to be your friend, you're so spiky and rude.'

'I know.' Flynn clenched his jaw. 'I know I've made lots of mistakes. I *know* I've done stupid, dangerous things. You don't need to keep reminding me.'

'Really?' I spat. 'Coming from someone who just spun around a car park on top of a car, I think you need reminding every second of every day.'

We glared at each other. Then Flynn's face creased into a smile. 'Mmm, you got me there.' He held out his hand. 'Come on, Riv, let's not fight.'

I shook my head. 'You can't just wash over it like that.' As I spoke I could feel my anger seeping away and a deep and terrible sadness taking its place.

'I knew what I was doing on the car,' Flynn insisted, letting his hand fall to his side. 'I *told* you I'd be all right and I was. Why didn't you trust me?'

'Because last year you said you loved me and you

187

went away and I don't see how I can trust you after that.' A huge sob rose inside me. It didn't matter how much Flynn had changed, or how much I loved him. I could never get away from the fact that he'd left me. A tear trickled down my cheek. 'It doesn't matter what your reasons were, you didn't love me enough to stay.'

Flynn gazed at me, his hair wet against his head, his eyes glistening. 'It wasn't that, Riv. I did love you, I *do.* I've never stopped.' His voice cracked. 'The real truth is that being with you was right, but everything else in my life was wrong. And because it was wrong I couldn't see straight and the reason I got so angry was part of the whole thing . . . I didn't think I was good enough to deserve your love.'

'That's a stupid way to look at it,' I muttered.

'I know,' Flynn said, 'but let's face it. I've got a lot of form for being stupid, as you've just pointed out.'

I laughed and reached for his hand. Suddenly I felt better. 'A year ago you'd have been furious if I'd said all that to you.'

Flynn took my hand and squeezed it hard. 'You're not the only one who's grown up, you know.'

I laughed again and we carried on walking along the winding cliff path. The rain teemed down as we reached the stony beach at the bottom. Clouds shrouded the moon, but the white tips of the waves lit up the sea as they sucked and spat pebbles back on to the ground.

As we walked along, I started shivering from the cold. My clothes were damp against my skin and my body ached with exhaustion. I tripped over a large stone and, though Flynn's arm around my shoulder prevented me from going flying, my ankle ached when I tried to put weight on it.

I limped for a few steps, then stopped. Flynn was peering at the beach ahead.

'What is it?' I asked.

'I just want to check something, wait here a sec.' Before I could say anything, Flynn vanished into the darkness. I sat down on the damp stones and felt my ankle. It wasn't badly hurt, but right now, as tired and cold as I was, it felt like the last straw.

A few moments later and Flynn was back. He held out his hand and pulled me to my feet.

'I'm afraid we can't get to Starhaven. At least, not right now.'

'What do you mean?'

'I mean that that the tide's coming in and we're going to be stuck in this bay until it goes out again,' he said.

19

I stared at Flynn. 'The tide's coming in?' I gazed up at the sheer rockface around the bay, my heart sinking at the thought of having to climb back up the cliff to escape the water. 'Are you sure?'

Flynn gazed out over the dark sea. It was broken only by small ripples of white. The bright lights of Starhaven shone in the distance.

'Yes,' he said.

The rain was still falling heavily. My hair was plastered to my face. I brushed it away, feeling like crying.

'It's like we're on a different planet,' I said, swallowing down a sob. 'A million miles away from everything. A million years.'

Flynn pulled me towards him. His hands on my back felt strong and warm. 'I don't care where I am, so long as you're here too.'

I held him tight as the rain poured down around us and on us. Thunder rumbled in the distance. I shuddered at the sound.

'It's like the world's ending,' I said.

Flynn held me more tightly.

'I wouldn't want to be in a world where you aren't,' he whispered.

We clung to each other as a crack of lightning flashed through the sky. Over Flynn's shoulder, the sudden blaze of white lit up the far corner of the beach. A dark shape loomed up, then vanished again as the lightning died away.

'What was that?' I pulled apart from Flynn and pointed to the end of the beach.

He followed my gaze as more lightning split the sky. This time we both saw it clearly.

'It's a hut,' Flynn said.

'Come on.'

He helped me hobble across the stones to the little wooden shed. Flynn yanked at the door. It swung open. We went inside. It was empty. Almost derelict in fact, with bare boards on the floor and walls and the wind whistling in between the slats. A blanket had been laid in the corner, next to a couple of candles and a box of matches.

'Looks like someone uses this place already,' Flynn said.

'Maybe that means the tide doesn't get this far up,' I said.

Flynn nodded. 'Yeah, you're right, otherwise this would be wet.' He held up the blanket, then spread it over our shoulders. 'Come on, at least this gets us out of the rain.'

We huddled together at the back of the hut. Flynn put his arm across my back, nudging my head down against his chest. 'Why don't you try and sleep,' he said. 'Or is your ankle hurting?'

'No, it's better now I'm not walking.' I tucked the blanket under me and nestled closer to him. We sat in silence. I had always marvelled at how easy it was for us to be together without speaking, as if the normal need for words to fill the void between two people just didn't apply to Flynn and me. Now I marvelled twice over at how this was still the same despite the fact that we hadn't seen each other for months.

As we sat, holding each other, I started to feel warm for what felt like the first time in hours. I yawned, my body rising and falling against his.

'Sleep, Riv,' Flynn murmured. 'Sleep. I'll stay awake . . . keep watch.'

'Keep the vampires from my door?' I smiled. 'Like in the song?'

'Yeah.'

'With your undying, death-defying love for me?'

'Go to sleep, Riv.'

I closed my eyes. And I slept.

I woke, feeling warm. The whole blanket surrounded me, pulled up over my head and down to my toes. For a moment I had no idea where I was, then all the memories of the day before rushed through me. My eyes sprang open. I was in a hut, on a beach. Strips of bright light shone in through the tiny gaps in the walls. Where was Flynn?'

I turned sharply, expecting him to be on my other side.

But he was gone.

'Flynn?' I sat up. '*Flynn?*'

No reply.

Blinking the sleep out of my eyes I struggled to my feet and hurried to the door. My ankle ached a little, reminding me of our clamber down the cliff last night, then all the terrible events that had preceded it.

I pushed open the door. Light flooded the hut, blinding me. I held my hand, shielding my eyes from the sunshine.

Wow. It was a beautiful morning. The sun was already high in a clear blue sky. I tilted my face up to its warmth for a second, then peered across the bay, looking for Flynn.

The tide had clearly risen then retreated again and the sea was now in the distance, leaving a long stretch of beach that led to the town we had been aiming for last night.

There he was – a thin, dark figure far away near the sea, silhouetted against the sun. He was bending over, picking something off the stones. Then he turned back, as if sensing me watching him.

He raised his hand. I waved back, then pushed my hair off my face. *Ugh.* It was all matted, in dry, salty clumps at the side where I'd slept on it. Flynn was walking back towards me now. I glanced down at my clothes. They were covered in dirt. So were my legs and arms. My face must be the same, as well as streaked with make-up. I stood, self-conscious that I must look truly hideous.

Flynn was running now. I held my breath, watching as he drew closer. He was so beautiful, all lean and muscular, with that perfect face. A bunch of seaweed dangled from his hand. What was that for?

A second later, he reached me, his eyes more green than gold in the bright light.

'It's beautiful here, isn't it?' he breathed, dropping the seaweed at my feet.

I drew back as he tried to kiss me. My stale breath would totally spoil the effect of this lovely morning.

'Don't. I look horrible,' I said.

Flynn blinked in surprise. 'Riv.' He hesitated. 'I don't know how to tell you just how beautiful you are to me. Right here. Right now. Always.'

I stared at him. 'Shut up, I'm a mess.'

'No.' Flynn took my face in his hands. He smoothed the skin under my eyes with his thumbs. 'I love you.'

I gazed into his eyes, my heart swelling. 'I love you back.'

We kissed, then Flynn bent down and picked up the bunch of seaweed. 'I got this for your ankle.'

He made me sit down, while he pressed the damp green fronds around the tender area. The seaweed felt wonderfully cool against my skin.

'Thank you,' I said.

He kissed me again. We sat on the stones, watching the tide come in and out.

'That wasn't quite the last night together I'd imagined,' he said softly.

I glanced across at him and in that moment all the trauma of the past twenty-four hours seemed to melt away. For the first time since Cody had forced me into his car, I felt at peace.

It wasn't the sparkling sea or the bright, fierce sun. And it wasn't knowing that here, on this beach in what felt like the middle of nowhere, we were safe.

It was being here with Flynn, without drama or trauma.

And in my heart I knew the truth, the clear, undeniable, powerful truth.

We belonged together. It was really that simple.

'Maybe we should give ourselves one more try at it,' I suggested, shyly. 'You know, have the whole of today and tonight, then go to the police tomorrow.'

Flynn's eyes lit up. 'D'you mean it?'

I nodded. We sat for a few moments longer, then wandered along the stony beach, keeping the tumbling waves on our right as we headed towards Starhaven. I was still limping a little, but I barely noticed, my heart was so full. A whole day more before I had to face the police. And reality.

We held hands and chatted as we walked. 'We'll buy some food as soon as we can,' Flynn said. 'I want two hamburgers and a big bag of chips.'

'I'd like a cheese sandwich and some lemonade. *Proper* lemonade,' I added. 'I'm so thirsty my tongue feels swollen.'

We rounded our bay, then the next. Starhaven was only a mile or so away now. As we wandered hand in hand, a tramp appeared in the distance. His hair hung long over a stained orange T-shirt and his trousers were tied at the bottom with string.

'D'you think it was his blanket we used in that hut?' I whispered.

'Maybe.' Flynn put his arm protectively around me.

The man gazed at us as we passed him. He had a thick beard and leathery-brown skin. His eyes were a striking pale blue with dark rings around the irises. He stopped as he saw Flynn.

'Hello,' he said, as if he knew him.

'Hi,' Flynn said uncertainly. His grip on my shoulder tightened.

I looked at the tramp. His hair was completely matted, but his face was clean and his eyes were calm. I was sure he didn't intend to hurt us.

'Hello.' I smiled.

The tramp glanced at me, then back to Flynn. He waved his hand in the air, as if gesturing to another person.

'Do you see him?' he asked Flynn, tilting his head to one side.

Flynn frowned. 'See who?'

There was a long pause. The waves crashed in my ears. The tramp sighed. 'Death,' he said. 'He's there, just behind you.' He pointed at an empty space on the beach behind Flynn. Then he moved closer so I could see the brown and yellow of his teeth. He smiled, like he meant to be friendly. 'He's in the shadows, waiting.'

Flynn's mouth gaped.

'Go away,' I said firmly.

The tramp ignored me. He was still gazing at the empty patch of beach.

'It won't be long,' he said, in a matter-of-fact way, as if he were talking about when the next bus might arrive.

Flynn and I stared at him, but he no longer seemed aware we were there. A moment later a seagull squawked overhead and he wandered away, leaving the two of us alone.

20

I turned to Flynn, feeling shaken.

'What a weirdo,' I said.

'Yeah.' Flynn shrugged. The shock had gone from his face, his expression now one of mild irritation. 'Probably high.'

'Right.' I looked at him carefully. Despite his apparent unconcern, I could see the shadow of anxiety behind his eyes. 'He was just some crazy guy, Flynn,' I said.

'Sure.' He smiled. 'I know.'

I took his hand and we walked on, along the beach. Soon I forgot all about the tramp. It was just so lovely to be with Flynn, the sea sparkling and the sun shining. My ankle still ached a little, but not enough to spoil the walk. All the bad stuff that had happened last night felt like it belonged to some horror film. I knew that I was going to have to face the whole drama of Cody and the shooting eventually – but that would be tomorrow. Today stretched ahead of us.

And tonight. A night in a proper room. Together.

As we neared Starhaven, Flynn checked his phone again. 'I've got a signal,' he said. 'D'you want to call your mum or dad again? I think they've left voice-mails.'

I took his phone and searched the call log. Three unidentified mobile numbers appeared as missed calls from last night. There were five voicemail messages. I handed the phone back to Flynn.

'I don't want to speak to Mum and Dad right now.'

Flynn peered at the call log. 'Whose is the third number?' he asked.

'Leo's, probably, but I can't be sure.' I sighed.

'Leo was calling you?' There was a sharp edge to Flynn's voice.

I looked up. He was frowning.

'I told you,' I said. 'We're friends. *Good* friends.' I thought of Leo's unhappy face when I'd told him I couldn't see myself ever going out with him. '*Just* friends.'

'He's in love with you, isn't he?' Flynn stopped walking and stared at me.

I hesitated. 'Maybe,' I said. 'Yes, he hasn't said it but I think he is.'

Flynn gave a low growl.

'But I don't love him, Flynn.' I took his hand. 'And I've *never* let him think I did. I—'

'It's not that.' Flynn frowned. 'Sorry, I didn't mean to make you think I was mad.' He kept hold of my hand as we started walking again. 'I was just thinking maybe you'd be better off with . . . with someone like Leo.'

My heart flipped over in my chest. 'No,' I said. 'That's not how it works. You can't choose who you love. The universe just tells you.'

Flynn snorted. 'You've spent too much time on that hippy commune, Riv.'

I grinned. 'Whatever, you're still stuck with me.'

We walked on. In the end I decided to send a text to all three phone numbers to reassure them I was still okay. My message just said:

Got delayed but I'm fine. Don't worry. Home tomorrow. Love Rxxx

I pressed send, then told Flynn to turn the mobile to silent, so we could ignore any further attempts to contact us.

A few moments later we reached the outskirts of Starhaven. We slipped inside the public toilets on the seafront car park. I was shocked by how grubby my clothes and face were. I did my best to wash off the worst of the dirt and to scrape my filthy hair into a ponytail.

'I so need a shower,' I said.

'Food first,' Flynn said. 'I'm beyond starving now.'

We found a little café just past the car park. Neither the burgers nor the sandwiches looked great, so we ate a breakfast of bacon, eggs and toast. My ankle was starting to feel sore again now, so we didn't waste any more time searching the area, but went into the first B & B we came too. Luckily it was perfect – clean and basic, with white curtains and wooden furniture. Our room was on the first floor overlooking the sea. We showered together, washing each other's hair. I made Flynn scrub at mine until the skin smarted.

After he'd finished he drew me close, kissing me as the water ran down our faces. Later, we sponged the worst of the dirt off our clothes, then lay down on the bed. We talked and we made love all afternoon. In the end we got hungry again. We didn't have much money left – just enough for fish and chips, which we ate on the harbour beach, looking out at the boats.

We finished as the sun set, then leaned against each other watching the moon over the water.

After a while I shivered and Flynn took my hand and led me back to the B & B. It had been a beautiful day and we had talked about everything that mattered – our friends and families and work and college. Everything except the future.

Back in our room, I brought the subject up. 'Tomorrow morning, should we go to the police ourselves, or call my dad first?'

'Your dad, I think,' Flynn said. 'Maybe he'll meet us at the police station. We can try and explain everything to him there.'

'Afterwards,' I went on, 'what do you think will happen? To you, I mean.'

Flynn shrugged. 'I'll probably be arrested for all the work I did for Bentham. I can try explaining I didn't know what he was involved with until he asked me to hide the first gun for him, but that was months ago. Even if I give them information on Bentham's operation, I'll probably be charged.' He sighed. 'And even if I plead guilty, it'll almost certainly be a custodial sentence.'

'You mean *prison*?' The possibility that Flynn might be arrested and charged had crossed my mind before, but I hadn't seriously thought he would end up in jail. 'How long for?'

Flynn shrugged again. 'Several years, I expect.'

'What?' I couldn't believe it. 'But you didn't *do* anything with the gun.'

'I hid it for people who did. Which makes me partly responsible for whatever *they* did.'

'It won't stop me seeing you,' I insisted.

Flynn hesitated. 'Maybe it should.' He frowned.

'Anyway, your parents definitely won't want you to.'

'I don't care.' I wandered to the window. It was hard to believe things would be so different tomorrow. 'I wish everything didn't have to change.'

'I know.' Flynn sat up on the bed. 'Let's not talk about it any more. Hey, I wish we had some music.'

I stared at him, suddenly remembering his present to me. 'We do.'

I fished the tiny iPod out of my pocket and we stood by the window, one earphone each, and swayed through all ten of Flynn's River songs, gazing out at the waves as they swept into the harbour. We danced until it grew dark outside. Afterwards we lay on the bed and kissed. Soon, I knew, it would be the last kiss before the spell broke and we had to face reality again. I held Flynn more tightly than ever as he whispered his feelings in my ear. I felt so full of love for him, and yet the shadow of tomorrow loomed over us – dark and threatening. And when we made love it was furiously, as if bombs were falling all around us and this was our final defiant act on earth.

I slept soundly, exhausted after the past forty-eight hours of tension and drama. And then, deep in the darkness of the night, something woke me: a noise or a feeling, I couldn't tell. But I sat bolt upright in the bed, gasping for air.

Flynn was already across the room, his ear pressed against the door.

'What is it?' I hissed.

He motioned me to be quiet with his hand, listened for a moment longer, then crept back to the bed. He sat down beside me. Moonlight shone in through a gap in the curtains, lighting one side of his face. I stared at the slope of his nose and the way his hair fell over his eyes. The scar where his dad had wounded him so many years before was a puckered line on his shoulder. My heart pummelled in my chest.

'I heard a noise,' Flynn whispered. 'Someone's downstairs in reception.'

I was wide awake now. 'Do you think it's Cody?' I gasped. 'How could he know we were here?'

Flynn said nothing, then he looked up. His eyes glinted like gold coins in the dim light. 'I'm going to check it out, Riv,' he whispered. 'Stay here. Lock the door after me. I'll come back.' He turned away, reaching for his top.

A shiver ran down my spine. Suppose it was Cody? Suppose he still had his gun? I caught Flynn's hand as he got off the bed.

'Promise me you'll come back,' I whispered.

'I promise,' he said. 'Promise me you'll stay here 'till I do?'

'Okay, I promise.' Before I could say anything else, he was across the room and out the door. He made no sound crossing the landing outside. I tiptoed to the door and peered out in time to see him vanishing down the stairs. I strained my ears, but I couldn't hear voices. Part of me wanted to follow him down to reception but my promise held me back. It was silly, but I felt somehow that if I broke my word and left the room, Flynn would somehow be prevented from keeping his promise to return.

I locked the door, checked it, then crept back to bed. Flynn's phone was gone from the side of the bed, but the B & B clock's neon figures showed the time was three a.m. Outside the sky was a dark grey, the first swirls of faintest pink just edging along the horizon. I shivered, pulling the covers over me, listening out for sounds from downstairs.

I couldn't hear anything. Time ticked away. Anxiety crept through my chest, tightening my breathing. Where was Flynn? Surely he'd been gone long enough to see who was downstairs in reception? If it was some random hotel guest or a member of staff, he would have come straight back. If it was Mum or Dad, there was no way they wouldn't be up here already. If it was Cody . . .

I didn't want to think about what Cody might do if Flynn confronted him. I had promised Flynn I would stay here, but maybe he needed my help. I counted out another sixty seconds in my head. That was it. I couldn't wait any longer. I had to see if he was all right. I threw the covers off and sat up. But, just as I swung my feet on to the wooden floor, a footstep creaked outside the door.

I froze. Someone was there.

21

I held my breath, watching the door. Terrified thoughts raced through my head. Maybe it *had* been Cody downstairs. Maybe he had seen Flynn and attacked him. Left him unconscious. Dead. Then crept silently up the stairs to find me.

A light tap on the door. I backed away, glancing around the room for something I could use to fend Cody off. There was nothing except the bedside lamp. That had a slim wooden stem; I couldn't see it being a very effective weapon. Could I jump out the window? We were on the first floor with a concrete pavement immediately below. I would probably break my legs if I jumped.

Another rap on the door, more firm this time. I reached for the lamp. It would have to do.

'River?' Flynn's urgent whisper sent relief flooding through my veins.

I set the lamp down and rushed to the door.

'River?'

I turned the key and Flynn came inside. As he shut the door behind him I flung my arms around him.

'Hey,' he said, sounding startled. 'What's the matter?'

'I thought Cody had found us,' I said, a huge sob welling inside me. 'I thought he was here, that he'd killed you.'

Flynn held me. He said nothing, just led me back to the bed. We sat under the covers, our arms around each other. At first I was so grateful he was alive, all I could do was hug him tightly. But after a minute or two it struck me that, although Flynn was hugging me back, he seemed more distant than when he'd left. I pulled away.

'What's going on?' I asked. 'Who was downstairs?'

'No one.' Flynn didn't meet my eyes. 'Just someone looking for something . . . I dunno . . . nothing.'

I frowned. 'You were a long time down there if it was nothing.'

Again, Flynn didn't speak. Anxiety swirled inside me. Something was wrong.

'Flynn, *please*, you're worrying me.'

He turned and met my gaze at last. I was shocked by the pain in his eyes. I opened my mouth to ask what was the matter, but before I could speak, Flynn leaned over and kissed my lips.

'You know I love you more than anything?' he murmured.

'Mmm.' The whisper-soft touch of his mouth set my whole body on fire. I put my hand to his face to draw him closer, but Flynn pulled away. He sat back against the pillows.

'We can't do this,' he said. His voice sounded hollow. Numb.

'Do what?' My chest tightened.

Flynn let out a long shaky breath. There was real agony in his eyes. 'I realised when I was downstairs. That's why I took so long, I was thinking it through. And it won't work, our plan,' he said.

'What do you mean? *What* won't work?'

'*None* of it will work: going to the police together. Telling your parents we want to be together again. *Being* together.'

'What?' I gasped. 'What are you saying? Don't you *want* to do those things any more?'

'Of course I do.' Flynn rubbed his forehead. 'It's just they won't work.'

'*Why* won't they work?' I persisted, my voice rising. 'You're not making sense.'

Flynn nodded. Then he took a deep breath. 'I want more than anything to be with you, Riv. But it's not fair on you. You saw Cody murder someone. That changes *everything*. You're going to have to make a statement, deal with police and lawyers. Face Cody in court, probably . . . It's going to drag on for months and I'll be in prison. You need your family and friends behind you.'

'And they *will* be behind me,' I said. 'I don't get you saying it isn't fair on me. We already agreed going to the police is the right thing to do.'

'It *is* the right thing,' Flynn acknowledged. 'But if we're together – a couple – when you do it, if we go back out together, then you'll have to deal with everyone else in your life disapproving. You'll be completely isolated.'

'No.' My voice rose again. '*No*, I'll have you. Won't I?'

'You'll always have me.' Flynn stared, miserably, into my eyes. 'And I'll always love you, Riv. *Always*.'

'What does that mean? It sounds like you're leaving. *Again*. When you promised you would stay with me, you said that you wanted to be with me forever.' I stopped, my voice too choked to speak. '*Are* you leaving?' I whispered.

There was a long, terrible silence. Then Flynn nodded. 'I have to,' he said. 'It's the best thing for you.'

He got off the bed and reached for his shoes. My head spun. How could this be happening? Before Flynn went downstairs everything had been fine.

As he stood up I caught sight of his phone, peeking out of his pocket.

'Did someone call you when you were downstairs?' I asked. 'Did you speak to someone?'

'I've written down the three numbers who called earlier,' Flynn said, ignoring me and pointing to a scrap of B & B headed paper lying on the bed. 'My number's there too, so you can reach me if you really need to. I'll call your mum and dad when I'm gone. Tell them what's happened, where you are . . .'

'Flynn, *please.*'

He swooped over me, one hand cradling my face, his lips swift and soft on my cheek. 'Always love you,' he whispered. 'It's in the stars. Remember.'

And then he left.

I couldn't move. Couldn't feel. I sat back against the pillows, the entire universe reeling, out of control, inside my head.

Outside the window the sky lightened. I stared and stared at the blue spreading through the pink.

He was gone.

22

I sat dry-eyed on the bed, watching the sun rise over the water. It was beautiful, yet its beauty didn't touch me. Flynn had gone. He had left me again. And, okay, so he had said this time that he loved me and didn't want to hurt me and was leaving because it was the best thing *for* me, but he had still come and gone and I had given up my heart to him and now it was smashed into a million pieces.

Again.

Two hours passed. The sun outside shone brightly in a clear blue sky. It was going to be another hot day. Yet whereas the glittering water had seemed so romantic yesterday, now it hurt my eyes to look at it.

I knew that I had to follow through with our plan to call the police. It was the right thing to do, though I had to admit I was scared to do it alone. Still, I told myself, I'd been alone for the past eight months. I had survived this long without him. I'd survive into the future.

I just wasn't sure whether I wanted to.

Another hour went by. I was hungry, but I didn't have the energy to eat. There was no money anyway. Flynn had left behind everything he had – but it would only just cover the B & B bill. What would *he* live on now? I sighed. If he kept his word and went straight to the police, then Flynn would be in custody right now and food and shelter would be the least of his problems.

I gathered up my few things. I hesitated over the iPod with the River songs but in the end I shoved it into my pocket. I didn't have to decide whether or not to keep it right now. I slipped on my shoes and picked up the piece of paper on which Flynn had scribbled all the mobile numbers. I would pay downstairs, then ask them if I could borrow their phone to call Mum and Dad.

Flynn had drawn a little star beside the one at the bottom. I knew that meant it was his number. A sob rose in my throat but I didn't let myself cry. There was no point. Just as there was no point in me calling him. No point in anything any more.

I took a deep breath and opened the door.

My parents stood outside. Dad's hand was raised, ready to knock. We stared at each other as Dad lowered his hand. Mum stood beside him, open-mouthed, her eyes smaller than usual without make-up. Dad's face screwed into an anxious frown.

'River?' he said.

'Oh, Dad.' I fell into his arms, letting him hug me. 'I'm sorry. I'm so, so sorry.'

Dad held me for a minute. He asked if I was okay and I said I was. Mum started bombarding me with questions but Dad raised his hand, gesturing her to stop, which she did. Dad then took me downstairs. I was dimly aware of Mum checking out the bedroom then following us. The B & B owner was bleary-eyed at the reception desk. It must still be very early. Dad apologised as he paid for the room. I offered him Flynn's cash but he refused it.

'Are you hungry?' Mum asked.

I shook my head. She stared despairingly at Dad.

'We'll get something on the motorway,' he said. 'Nothing's open yet anyway.'

They bundled me into the back seat of Dad's old estate car. The baby car seat was on its side next to me. I remembered Lily with a guilty jolt.

'Is she okay?' I asked, as Dad started the engine. 'Is Gemma?'

'They're both fine,' Dad said tersely. 'Though Gemma's worried about you. Like we all are.'

I nodded. 'Mum. Dad,' I said. 'I have to go to the

police.' The image of Cody shooting the man in the car park reared up in my mind's eye.

'We know,' Mum said.

'Flynn called and explained what happened,' Dad said. His voice was tight and strained. 'Why didn't you tell us you'd seen him?'

I turned my face to look out of the window and said nothing.

Dad sighed. 'Okay, this is what we're going to do,' he said firmly. 'We'll drive to a service station. Stop. Eat. You tell us exactly what happened. Then we go to the police station near to where you saw . . . the shooting.'

'I don't know exactly where it was,' I said.

'Flynn told us,' Mum said.

The way she said his name made my heart shrivel.

Tears welled in my eyes. I huddled in the corner of the back seat and wept in silence. I had never felt so alone.

23

The police officer was very understanding. I sat, with Mum and Dad on either side, as she asked me to start from the beginning, from the first time I'd met Cody.

I told her about seeing him at the wedding, then at the party. I explained how I'd overheard him and Flynn arguing in the garden, then how, a week later, I'd gone to find Flynn 'to return his wallet'.

At this Mum tutted and Dad sighed. I couldn't bear the look of disappointment on their faces, so I hurried on, telling them how Cody had tricked me into the back room, how I'd escaped, then how I'd seen a man give him money to kill someone.

'Could you identify this man?' the policewoman asked.

'No, I didn't see his face,' I admitted. 'But I'm sure it was Lance Bentham.'

The policewoman looked at her colleague, then back at me. 'Go on,' she said.

I described how Flynn had come to warn me that Cody was trying to track me down. 'Cody was scared I'd go back to the police, give a proper statement,' I explained.

'Why didn't you tell us?' Mum said.

I shrugged. 'I thought you'd be mad I'd been in touch with Flynn.' I turned to Dad. 'You were so worried about Lily, I didn't want to upset you.'

Dad shook his head. There were tears in his eyes.

'I'm sorry,' I said. And I really meant it. 'I'm truly sorry I've let you down.'

Mum patted my arm. She looked as if she was restraining herself – with great difficulty – from telling me she'd been right about Flynn all along.

'Well at least Flynn's gone now,' she said. 'The whole thing is behind you.'

I bit my lip.

'All you need to focus on now is your statement, then we can take you home,' Dad added.

The police officer questioned me for another hour or so. She spent most of the time asking me to describe exactly what happened in the car park. I told her everything as best I could, emphasising how Cody had been threatening me, how I didn't think he had meant to kill the man he shot, and how Flynn had tried to save me.

At last it was done.

Dad took me home. Mum stayed while I had a bath and got into bed, then she left too. I didn't want to see anyone else at the commune that night. I was hurting too badly.

Instead, I played the River songs over and over – they seemed to sum up everything. After a while I took the heart bracelet Flynn had given me last year and buried it under the loose floorboard by the window. A few minutes later Dad came in. He perched on the edge of my bed and, after checking I was okay, explained that he and Gemma had decided to move into Leo's old apartment as soon as Leo and his dad left.

'There'll be more room for you and for Lily there,' he said. 'I'm going to build a new room out of a corner of the living room, then extend the living room into the hallway. There's a lot of wasted space there right now.'

I let him talk on, describing their plans. I nodded and asked a few questions. I knew my priority was to make sure Dad believed I was all right. I had upset him so much last year when Flynn left the commune. I was determined never to be that selfish again.

'That means you'll have Leo's room,' Dad said.

'Right.' I thought about the room with its wall covered in pictures and the window seat overlooking the field. 'That's great, it's a lovely room.'

'It is,' Dad agreed. He cleared his throat. 'Leo's been asking after you. Do you feel up to seeing him?'

'Not right now,' I said. 'Maybe tomorrow.'

Dad frowned. 'I was hoping you'd come down for dinner later, you know, in the kitchen?'

'Right.' My heart sank. A communal supper was the last thing I wanted tonight. Still, I had to look after Dad. 'The others won't ask me about Cody or the police, will they?'

'I'll make sure they don't,' Dad said firmly.

I nodded. If I was going to have to face everyone later, I might as well see Leo beforehand. I shoved the iPod under my pillow.

'Is Leo in his room?' I asked.

'I think so,' Dad said.

I swung my legs off the bed. 'I'll go and see him now.'

Dad looked pleased.

I trudged along the corridor to Leo's apartment. The front door was open so I slipped inside. Ros and Leo's dad were sitting with their arms around each other in the living room, watching TV.

'Hey, River.' Ros jumped up and embraced me in a hug.

'Hi,' I said, feeling awkward. Since falling for Leo's dad, Ros had become far more tactile than before and I still wasn't used to it. She tried to get me to sit with them, but I pulled away. 'I just want a word with Leo,' I said.

'Sure.' Ros sat down, nodding vigorously. 'Sure, just so long as you're okay.'

'I'm fine,' I said.

I walked along to Leo's room and tapped lightly on the door. There was no reply, so I gently opened it. Leo was sitting cross-legged on the bed, a text-book open in his lap and a steady beat pulsing through the headphones clamped to his ears. He was murmuring along to the song he was listening to. I watched him for a moment. Leo had phenomenal powers of concentration. He was smart too. Not carelessly, confidently smart like Flynn who had always got excellent results by simply doing what was needed with the minimum of fuss. No, Leo was more like an absent-minded professor, working hard because he loved to find out about things, because he wanted to learn for its own sake.

I came inside and shut the door. Leo didn't see me until I moved across the room. Then he caught my shadow and looked up. He smiled, taking off his headphones. And there was so much genuine affection and relief in his smile that I couldn't help but smile back in spite of my misery. On instinct, I opened my arms and Leo leaped off the bed to hug me. We clung to each other for a moment. Leo was slighter and shorter than Flynn, but he had broadened out in the past few months and, right now, he felt solid and safe.

'I want us to be friends,' I said.

Leo drew back. 'Of course,' he said. 'We are.'

'Even when you move to Devon?' I said. 'Even though you hate me because of Flynn?'

'Yes, and I don't hate you.' Leo rolled his eyes. 'I *care* about you.'

I hugged him again. 'I know. I'm sorry if I got angry with you before. Everything you said was true and before you ask I don't want to talk about what's happened in the past few days. Deal?'

Leo considered for a moment. 'Deal,' he said.

I wandered over to the window seat. From here I could just make out the roof of the barn where Flynn and I had split up eight months ago.

I turned away. I wasn't going to think about Flynn.

Leo was still standing beside his bed. I hadn't been in here for ages and Leo had added to the photos he'd taken on the wall. He had a good eye and there were lots of great pictures, particularly of the sea. Something else was different today.

Normally there was a gap in the pictures by the bed, but today the gap was filled with a photo.

It was a photo of me. Taken last summer, it showed my head and shoulders against the backdrop of the apple orchard. I only vaguely remembered Leo snapping it.

'I'd forgotten you took that,' I said.

Leo followed my gaze. 'Damn,' he said. 'I didn't mean you to see I had that there – normally I take it down before you come round.'

I stared at him. 'You keep a photo of me by your bed?'

Leo rolled his eyes. 'Don't make it sound so creepy. It's a beautiful photo.'

I peered closer. It *was* a nice picture. 'Makes me look like I have cheekbones,' I said.

'It's just you,' he said. He looked away.

I hesitated, embarrassed. I'd so hoped Leo and I really could be friends after all, but the way he was acting now suggested he still had romantic feelings. Maybe I'd been stupid to think they would have gone so fast. After all, I was still in love with Flynn after almost two whole years.

Leo was still staring out of the window. He looked so miserable that it was all I could do to stop myself reaching over and hugging him again. But I sensed that would only make the situation

223

worse. And Leo's life was hard enough: his mum was dead, he wasn't really close to his dad and he didn't fit in at college. He'd once told me he'd been bullied at every school he'd attended. I was his closest friend and I had barely been there for him for the past few weeks. The very least I owed him was a bit of my time.

'So what's new?' I asked, hoping to change the subject.

'Nothing much.' Leo hesitated, his face clouding over. 'I spoke to Flynn earlier, you know.'

I stared at him. 'Did you?' I said, startled. 'How did—'

'I called the number you'd rung your mum on. Your dad did too. But nobody answered.'

I nodded, remembering all the missed calls and the third number logged on Flynn's mobile. 'I didn't know for sure you'd rung me,' I said. 'I'd lost my own phone and—'

'I know.' Leo waved his hand, as if to indicate explanations weren't needed. 'The point is that I was up half last night worrying about you and I kept ringing and ringing and eventually Flynn answered.'

'What did he say?' My heart felt like it was lodged in my throat.

'A few things,' Leo said. 'Like "Look after

224

River" . . . "She's the most amazing person I've ever met" . . . "I'm a waste of space" . . .'

I frowned. 'Seriously, Leo, you're saying Flynn told you he was a waste of space?'

'Okay, no, but he *did* say to look after you and that you were amazing and . . . and when I told him he was a jerk he didn't contradict me.'

'Right.' I turned to face the window. The sun was already low in the sky. Hours had passed since Flynn had left the hotel this morning. It felt like days already, yet the pain seared through me, fresh and sharp as a knife. Was it always going to be like this? Me missing Flynn so hard I couldn't breathe? I thought back to the last time I'd seen him, that miserable look in his eye. His decision to leave had come just after he'd gone outside our room to investigate a noise.

What if Leo had rung while Flynn was downstairs? What if it had been Leo's anger that had prompted Flynn to leave me?

'When *exactly* did you call him?' I demanded.

'I don't remember.' Leo shrugged. 'Just that it was the middle of the night.'

I glanced at the picture of me on his wall, suddenly seeing the whole thing. 'You told Flynn to leave me alone.'

'No, I didn't. I told you, I just said he was a jerk for getting you mixed up in—'

'You're lying,' I said. 'You thought if you made him leave me, then I'd fall in love with you.'

'What?' Leo said. 'That's *mad*. I said what I said because I *care* about you. Open your eyes, River. Flynn is a criminal. Thanks to him, you've been kidnapped, seen someone killed . . .' He paused. 'The only good thing Flynn's ever done was leave. *That* was right . . . for you and for your future.'

'How dare you tell me what's right for me and my future?' My fury rose with my voice. 'You say you're my friend, but you don't understand how it feels to love someone like I love Flynn.'

'Don't I?' Leo's mouth trembled slightly.

There was a knock on the door. Dad appeared, his face wreathed in anxiety. 'River, are you okay?'

'I'm fine,' I said, looking at the floor.

Dad cleared his throat. 'I just came over to . . . to tell you that Cody has been arrested.'

'Good,' I said. It was good, though right now I couldn't feel any relief. All I could feel was misery and anger – with Leo for interfering, with Flynn for listening and most of all with myself, for caring.

'I'm going back to our flat,' I said.

'Okay.' Dad gazed anxiously from me to Leo, then back to me. 'Are you sure everything's okay?'

'Yes,' I said. And I followed Dad out of the room without looking back.

24

A long week passed. I got myself a new phone and thought about calling Flynn. He had left me his number and said I should contact him if I needed anything, so it wasn't like before, when I'd thought he hated me. But every time I went to make the call, I stopped myself.

Flynn hadn't left because he didn't love me but because he was trying to protect me. I couldn't see him changing his mind. Whatever Leo had said to him – and I was still sure he had had a hand in Flynn leaving, despite his denials – had clearly convinced Flynn that keeping his distance was the best thing he could do for me.

I also learned that, despite what he'd said, Flynn had not after all gone to the police and told them about his work for Bentham. I didn't know what to make of that. He had been so adamant that he was ready to take responsibility for his mistakes that it was hard to believe he was prepared to go back on that now.

Mum and Dad, of course, thought I was being hopelessly naïve to have even expected Flynn to turn himself in.

'He's a lost cause,' Dad said wearily.

'More like a hardened criminal,' Mum said with a sniff. 'Leopards don't change their spots.'

I said nothing, but I was sure there was more to it than that.

My term at sixth form college was drawing to an end. Most people were excited about the long summer holiday stretching ahead. Personally, the prospect of endless weeks spent wandering around the commune helping out with all the usual chores filled me with a flat, sad sense of boredom. About the only thing that kept me going was having Lily in my life. Her sweet face and huge brown eyes never failed to make me smile and I spent a lot of time looking after her for Dad and Gemma.

Meanwhile Leo, his dad and Ros were planning to leave in August and move to a rented place in Devon while they looked for a permanent home. Leo was enrolled in a school down there, his third in as many years. Under other circumstances, I would have felt sorry for him but I was still too mad at him for warning Flynn off me – and for not having the guts to admit it.

Of course, the truth was that I was really mad at Flynn for listening – and at myself for not being smart enough to have found a way to make him stay. But, during those warm weeks at the end of June and the start of July, my anger stayed firmly directed at Leo. I hadn't been back to London since the night of that party in central London. I'd messaged with Grace and Emmi, but I hadn't told them about Flynn – or our ordeal with Cody. Of course they found out. Flynn had, apparently, called James and ordered him to keep an eye on me. I didn't know whether to feel irritated that he was still trying to oversee my life or touched by his concern.

The week college finished for summer, Grace called me, all excited about some holiday cottage belonging to friends of James's parents.

'We're going next weekend,' she said. 'What do you think?'

I hadn't followed half of what she'd said. These days my mind seemed to find it hard to focus. I wasn't letting losing Flynn eat away at me like I had before, but it still seemed to take all my energy to keep my misery at bay.

'Where is the cottage?' I asked.

'The Cotswolds,' Grace explained. 'It'll be just us. James is borrowing some huge car to drive us there, and there's plenty of room in the cottage. You'll love it.'

'Me?'

Grace gave an exasperated sigh. 'Yes, River. *You.* That's what I'm asking – will you come with us?'

'I'm not sure,' I said. A weekend away with James and Grace was the last thing I felt like facing. Not that they acted all loved-up any more, but they were still a couple. 'Will it just be the three of us?'

'For goodness sake, weren't you listening to anything I said?' Grace tutted. 'There'll be a whole bunch of people. Emmi and her boyfriend and one of his mates, plus a couple of others. Mostly people you know already. Please say yes.'

'Fine.' I agreed, mostly to get her off my back. What did it really matter where I spent the weekend? At least if I was away from the commune I wouldn't have to face all the concerned looks I got daily from the other residents here. Plus, much as I loved my new baby sister, it would be nice for once not to be woken several times a night by her crying.

Dad was delighted that I was heading off for the weekend, even giving me money towards James's petrol costs which I earmarked immediately for chocolate and alcohol.

By the time I'd packed a bag containing a couple of spare tops, some jewellery and my make-up, I was actually quite excited about the prospect of going away. Maybe this was the best thing for me after all. The court case with Cody, where I was going to have to give evidence as a witness, wouldn't take place for months. I was all set for my courses next year. I didn't expect to make any new friends over the weekend but at least I could try and forget my troubles with some old ones.

Towards the end of Friday afternoon, Gemma shouted up to tell me that James and the others had arrived. I raced downstairs to find Grace waiting by the door, a big smile on her face. I lugged my bag towards her, feeling better than I had done for weeks.

'Where's Leo?' Grace said, looking around. 'Isn't he ready?'

I stared at her. *'Leo?'*

Grace's smile faded. 'Didn't he tell you? James and I thought you'd like him to come, seeing as he's pretty much your bestie these days.' She winked at me. 'Oh, well, I guess he wanted to surprise you.'

'Right.' My heart sank. The last thing I needed was Leo along for the weekend.

Someone in the car outside sounded the horn – an impatient series of toots. Grace rolled her eyes.

'I'll go and tell them you won't be long.' She disappeared.

I heard footsteps behind me and turned.

'Hey, River.' It was Leo. He had a bag in his hand and a guilty expression on his face.

'Hi.' I raised my eyebrows.

'Er, River, I . . . er . . .' he stammered.

Outside, the car horn tooted again.

'I hear James invited you along,' I said.

Leo looked away. 'It was a last-minute thing,' he mumbled miserably. 'James only called me this morning. He and Grace have no idea we . . . they think we're still friends. I didn't know how to tell them I was the last person you'd want along for the weekend. They kind of insisted I came too. Thought I might be able to help cheer you up.' He made a face.

'It's fine,' I said, feeling awkward. 'Why didn't you say something earlier?'

'Because I was worried you'd hate the idea.' Leo sounded close to tears. 'Please, River, I can't stand that we're not speaking. I swear I didn't order Flynn to leave you alone or anything like it. He'd never listen to what I said anyway. You *know* he wouldn't.'

With a jolt I realised that this was true. That it was so obviously true I couldn't believe I hadn't faced up to the truth of it before. Flynn would never do something just because another person told him to. Especially Leo.

232

'Okay.' I forced a smile on to my face. 'I'm sorry, Leo, and it's fine you coming. More than fine.'

Leo was beaming as we headed out to the car. I wished I could feel happy too, but accepting at last that Flynn had decided to leave me of his own accord was hard to bear.

The cottage was lovely. I even almost enjoyed the journey there. I'd sat at the back of the nine-seater car with Emmi, her boyfriend – a good-looking, nineteen-year-old called Freddie – and his best friend, Sam, leaving Leo to ride with a couple of Grace's mates from school. James and Grace sat up front, bickering over the satnav like an old married couple.

Freddie and Emmi spent most of the ride all over each other, giving Sam and me a chance to talk. I liked him. I could even imagine, under other circumstances, being prepared to go out with him. He had sparkling blue eyes, a shock of wild, dark hair and a large nose that somehow fitted his face. Best of all he was confident and easy to talk to, making me laugh with his asides about James's driving and Freddie and Emmi's non-stop kissing.

Once we were inside the cottage – a little cream-coloured house on the outskirts of the Cotswolds and surrounded by sunlit fields – Freddie produced two large bottles of spiced vodka and suggested a game of strip poker. Grace and her friends looked so horrified that Emmi started laughing and her helpless giggles set me off too. The idea was dropped soon after, but Freddie then proceeded to mix a huge bowl of punch which appeared to contain every type of alcohol in existence, the flavours all covered over with masses of peach juice.

Leo kept trying to catch my eye. It was obvious that he disapproved of both Emmi and her boyfriend. I kept ignoring him. We'd already divided up rooms – Emmi and I had said we would share the basement bedroom, with Freddie and Sam on sofas in the living room. The others were all going to be upstairs. I was well aware that once the others had gone to bed, Emmi and Freddie would peel off, leaving me with Sam.

I decided to sleep with him. It would be part of my getting over Flynn. I'd hardly even kissed anyone apart from Flynn and had no idea what being with someone else would be like. Now seemed as good a time as any to find out.

Grace and one of her friends cooked up the pizzas we'd brought with us and everyone settled in the living room to watch a horror movie and drink Freddie's punch. Apart from a bit of tension between James and Freddie, late afternoon turned into evening without any real drama. Leo sat, silently, in a corner. He didn't look like he was having much fun but then Leo was always best one-on-one, tending to lose what little confidence he had in company.

And then Dad rang. I slipped outside to take the call. It was almost nine p.m. and the sun was slowly setting behind the garage that stood across the gravel from the cottage. I stood, watching the pinks and golds of the sky beyond the distant fields.

'River?' Dad sounded tense.

'What's up?' I asked. I'd already had two large glasses of the punch and was feeling pleasantly mellow.

'I've got some bad news.' Dad hesitated.

My chest tightened. Was this about the baby? Dad sounded more worried than distraught. 'What is it?'

'Cody has been released from custody, all charges dropped,' Dad said.

25

My insides seemed to shrivel up. '*What?*' I sucked in my breath, shocked to my core. 'How can they just let him go?'

'I don't know,' Dad said miserably. 'I just got the call from the police liaison person. Apparently there's not enough evidence to prosecute.'

'But . . . but I was *there*,' I said. 'I saw him shoot that man. And there must be CCTV or . . . or DNA traces too.'

'The CCTV doesn't show the shooting,' Dad explained. 'There was never any real evidence against Cody except your testimony.'

He paused and I knew he was thinking about Flynn's failure to turn himself in.

'What about the guys who saw us leave?' I asked.

'The cops can't trace them.'

'But . . .' My head spun. 'Why isn't my word enough?'

I could hear Dad taking a deep breath. 'They've decided your evidence isn't sufficiently strong. It's because of what happened last year . . . you spending that week in bed not talking, seeing the counsellor afterwards. They're saying you're not a reliable witness.'

'No,' I breathed.

'I'm so sorry, River.' Dad paused. 'I'm wondering if that gangster Cody and Flynn worked for – Bentham – has got something to do with this. Maybe he's put pressure on someone somewhere.'

I shivered. That was exactly what Flynn had predicted.

I spoke to Dad a little more. He emphasised that the police were monitoring Cody's movements. 'They've got someone following him right now,' he said.

I reassured him that I was fine, then I went back inside. The scene was the same as when I'd left, but now the whole party atmosphere seemed trivial and tacky. Freddie was again urging everyone to play strip poker and, though Emmi was the only person who appeared to think this was a good idea, neither of them were shutting up about it.

Deeply regretting my earlier decision to ally myself with them and Sam, who was already drunk,

I crept around the outskirts of the room, hoping no one would notice me as I headed upstairs.

I found a room and sat on the bed at its centre. It was a plain room, just a white duvet on the bed and no ornaments of any kind. It suited my bleak mood. After everything I'd been through, to know that Cody wasn't going to be prosecuted and sent to prison was the last straw.

I put my head in my hands. I wanted to cry, but the tears wouldn't come, so I just sat, listening to the music and laughter that drifted up from downstairs.

'At least you won't have to testify in court.' It was Leo.

I looked up. He was standing in the doorway, an expression of sympathy on his face.

'Your dad called,' he said, holding out his phone to explain how he'd heard the news. 'I'm so sorry, Riv.'

I bristled. Only Flynn was allowed to call me Riv. 'Go away.' I could hear my voice was like ice.

Leo blinked. 'River, I'm sorry, I thought you might want to talk.'

'I don't,' I said. 'Not to you.'

Leo gasped. I looked down, fury roiling inside me. I knew I was being desperately unfair. Cruel, in fact. It wasn't right to take my anger out on Leo. None of this was his fault.

'Right.' Leo was still in the doorway. I looked up. He was gazing at me, a look of total misery on his face.

Suddenly I felt mean. Disgusted with myself. I jumped up and ran over. 'I'm sorry, Leo. I didn't mean that. It's just . . .'

He put his arms around me. It was good to be held. Maybe I should sleep with Leo instead of Sam. I hugged him back.

For goodness sake. What was I thinking? Sleeping with Leo would only hurt him more. And it wasn't what I wanted at all. I should just be by myself.

With a sigh I pulled away.

'This is my room,' Leo said eagerly. 'You can sleep here too if you like.' He hesitated. 'Or you can just have it.'

'We can share it,' I said. 'As *friends*.' I peered into Leo's eyes to make sure he understood. 'Share the bed, right, but that's all?'

'Okay.' He nodded happily. 'I'll get your stuff from downstairs.'

'No rush.' I managed a smile. 'It's only nine o'clock.'

'Right, yeah.' Leo looked crestfallen.

For a second, I wondered if I was doing the right thing offering to share his room. Still, I'd made it clear nothing was going to happen.

We went back downstairs and I was instantly pleased that I wasn't going to end up with the others in the basement or on the sofas overnight. All the punch was gone and Freddie, Emmi, Sam and both Grace's friends were clearly totally drunk. They were playing some ridiculous game involving imitations of farmyard animals and a bottle of tequila.

I looked at Sam. He was so off his head that his eyes were glazed over and he was staring lustfully at the shorter of Grace's two friends. Thank goodness I'd changed my mind about sleeping with him.

He told us with a slurred sneer that Grace and James had gone outside for a walk. Leo and I glanced at each other, then decided to go outside ourselves.

It was a mild evening and we sat on the gate of a nearby field, watching the stars slowly fill the sky as darkness fell over the countryside. We talked properly for the first time in ages. Whatever his true feelings, at least now Leo was speaking as if we were friends. *Just* friends. He even mentioned liking a girl he'd met on his visit to his new sixth form college in Devon. Of course, being Leo, he was quite low key about it, but I felt hopeful that it was a sign he was, perhaps, genuinely starting to move on from his crush on me.

By the time we went back inside the cottage it was

past ten o'clock and properly dark. Sam and one of Grace's friends were kissing on the sofa. Grace and James were watching TV holding hands, with Grace's other mate looking very disgruntled beside them. There was no sign of Emmi and Freddie. I was guessing they had disappeared downstairs, into the basement bedroom.

Leo and I got ourselves some cold pizza from the fridge and sat at the kitchen table to eat it. After a while James and Grace joined us and we all chatted together for a while.

It was nice. Yet, though I felt calmer than I had done earlier, there was still a dull, depressed weight inside me.

Leo and James and Grace were all lovely but my soul was with Flynn, wherever he was, whatever he was doing. I ached with longing to see him, to feel his kiss on my lips and his fingers gently stroking my face, whispering how much he loved me in my ear.

I sat back with a sigh. How was I ever going to survive the rest of my life without him? Was it always going to feel like this: small and limited and dull? How could anyone else ever make me feel alive like Flynn did?

I took my drink and wandered over to the window. It was pitch black outside, only a few

241

lights twinkling from houses in the distance. And then my phone beeped. I glanced at it, assuming it was from Dad, with some sort of update on the Cody situation.

But it was from Flynn.

26

I stared at my phone, reading and rereading the text.

It's me. I'm outside. I need to speak to you. Please come. After everything I wouldn't ask if it wasn't important. Fx

Flynn was here? *Outside?*

I couldn't believe it, and yet the text was from the number he'd given me, *his* phone. I peered through the window again. It was pitch black outside, just the light from the house casting spooky shadows across the gravel. There was no sign of anyone out there. Anxiety crawled across my skin, making me shiver.

'Is everything all right?' Leo asked from across the kitchen.

I turned to face him, but I barely saw him. My heart was thundering in my ears.

'It's fine,' I said, forcing a smile on to my face. 'I just need some air.'

'And some company?' Leo asked hopefully.

I caught Grace and James exchanging a look across the table.

'Thanks, Leo, but no. I just want a minute outside alone.' I sped away before he could say any more. Music was blaring out from the living room, Sam and Grace's friend were still making out on the sofa. They didn't look up as I raced past to the front door. As I opened it, my phone beeped again.

I'm going away, Riv. Abroad. I just want to say goodbye. I'm in the garage. Fx

I glanced across the gravel to the garage. Light from the door I'd just opened cast a narrow path from the house, past James's car, to the garage door. The garage itself was still in darkness.

Why was Flynn being so mysterious? Well, the answer to that was obvious. He wouldn't want to muscle in on the entire weekend without speaking to me alone first. He must know that he wouldn't really be welcomed by any of the others, not even James.

As I hesitated, the inside of the garage lit up. Light spread out like a pool from the door, illuminating the gravel beyond. A five-pointed star had been drawn in the pebbles. Flynn had drawn a star just like that on Dad's car window.

All my reservations about seeing him vanished.

He was here, just a few metres away, waiting for me. I couldn't turn my back.

I closed the door quietly behind me and raced across the gravel to the garage. The door was pulled shut, not properly closed. I pushed it open and peered inside.

'Flynn?' I whispered.

No reply.

I took another step through the door. 'Flynn?' I whispered again.

'Here.' The voice spoke in a low whisper. I turned towards its sound.

And then a dark figure loomed over me, the light went out and Cody slapped his hand over my mouth, silencing the scream that rose in my throat.

27

Cody dragged me backwards across the garage floor. I kicked and punched at him, but he was too strong. I tried to yell, but his gloved hand over my mouth muffled the sound. My fingers clawed at his. Panic filled me. I couldn't tear him away. His skin smelled of stale cigarettes, his cheek rough and cold against my face.

'Quiet!' he hissed. He held me tightly against him. The tough leather of his jacket pressed against my back. He dug his fist against my stomach. There was something in his hand. I looked down, on to the barrel of a gun.

I froze.

Panting, Cody spun me around. He pointed the gun at my chest and swore.

'You stupid, stupid bitch,' he whispered. The venom in his voice made me shiver.

He walked me back, into the corner of the garage.

246

I glanced around. A low shelf stood on one side of me. It was full of drills and screwdrivers and bits of wood. On the other side a black tarpaulin lay crumpled on the floor. Cody pushed me back against the wall. It was cold through my top.

'Flynn.' His name slipped out of me in a sob.

'Oh don't you worry.' Cody raised his gun so that the barrel rested against my neck. 'I'm going after him too, make sure he pays for helping you run away from me. The pair of you have ruined my life. Bentham's cut me loose, the police are on my case.'

I stared into his mean grey eyes. 'But you're free,' I stammered. 'I don't understand, the police dropped all charges.'

'They're just waiting for me to slip up again,' Cody spat. 'It's *your* fault they arrested me in the first place.'

'If . . . if you hurt me, you'll be caught . . .'

'Will I?' A nasty smile curled around Cody's lips. 'No one knows I'm here. And this is Flynn's gun.'

I glanced down at the pistol. 'Flynn's?'

Cody nodded. 'The one he was hiding for Bentham. Didn't he explain how it works? Bentham and people like him . . . they don't keep their guns *with* them, they keep people to hold them, people who have to be on standby, ready to deliver the gun where and when it's needed at a moment's notice.'

'Flynn told me about that,' I stammered. 'He said he had done that . . . and that he's stopped.'

'Did he?' Cody shrugged. 'Well he's back to it now. Bentham's dumped me and given Flynn his job back. I took this gun from Flynn's place just two hours ago along with his phone.' He paused. 'That's how I figured out about the star thing. He'd drawn your name and this address with all these stars around it, the numpty.'

He studied my face. Desperate thoughts raced through my head. If only I could get away, back to the house, raise an alarm somehow. If only someone, Leo, would come to look for me. If only I hadn't said I wanted to be on my own.

'What are you going to do?' I stammered.

Cody moved closer until he was right in front of me, then he narrowed his cold grey eyes. 'I don't know what Flynn sees in you,' he murmured.

I shivered at the sneering menace in his voice.

'I love him,' I said. 'And he loves me.'

Cody shook his head. 'Love is for idiots.' He stroked the side of the gun up my face, pressing the metal against my temple. I froze with fear. This was it. He was going to kill me.

'Stop!' The garage door slammed open.

Keeping the gun against my head, Cody spun around.

Flynn stood in the doorway.

Our eyes met for a second. His shone gold in the light from above the door, terrified yet determined. I had a sudden flashback to the moment he came up to me after the audition when we met – how his presence filled the room like thunder in a dark sky and how his smile was like sunlight breaking through the clouds. A new strength filled me.

Flynn held up his hands. 'I called the police,' he said, his eyes on Cody. 'They'll be here any second. Let her go, Cody. You *have* to let her go.'

Cody said nothing, just pulled me back, further into the shadows at the very end of the garage. Flynn flicked on the overhead light, then followed us.

'Get back!' Cody warned.

'No.' Flynn walked towards us. 'You're a coward taking this out on River. She hasn't done anything wrong.'

'She ratted me out. Now Bentham won't have anything to do with me.'

'So find someone new to work for.' Flynn stopped a metre in front of us, his eyes on the gun at my throat. 'River saw you kill someone in that car park. You can't expect her to keep quiet about it. She doesn't work like that.'

'*You* kept quiet.'

Flynn's eyes flickered over my face. He was

checking that I was okay. I gave him a brief, reassuring nod.

'I kept quiet to keep River safe,' Flynn said in a low voice. He turned to me. 'That's the real reason why I left that night, Riv. I meant what I said about you being better off alone but there was more to it than that.'

I stared at his desperate face. 'What d'you mean?'

'Bentham came to our B & B,' Flynn went on. 'He'd tracked us through my phone. He did a deal with me. If I agreed to say nothing about what I knew about him to the police, if I went back to work for him, then he would let you alone.'

I gasped. 'I thought it was Leo you spoke to.'

Flynn frowned. 'I did speak to Leo, but not then.'

I bit my lip. So Leo had been telling the truth – and Flynn had lied to protect me.

'So what if Bentham did a deal with you,' Cody snarled. 'He left me hanging out to dry thanks to her evidence. That was *your* fault.'

'Come on, Cody,' Flynn pleaded. 'Bentham just got the police to drop all the charges against you.'

'So? That wasn't for me, that was for him, because he knew I could dump him in it.'

'So what? You're free aren't you?' Flynn took a small step towards us. 'But you won't be free for long if you hurt River.'

He turned to me. 'I've been checking in on you, making sure you were okay. I heard James was planning to come here and I followed you all down.' He looked at me – his eyes as intense as I'd ever seen him. 'I won't let Cody hurt you, I swear it.'

There was a long pause. My heart hammered in my chest. Then Cody shook his head. 'She's a bitch,' he said. 'She dies.'

'No,' Flynn insisted.

He took another step towards us. Cody cocked his gun. Flynn stopped.

I held my breath. Outside, a car engine sounded in the distance, its wheels turning slowly, scrunching over the gravel drive.

'People are here,' I said.

'It's the police,' Flynn insisted.

Cody pressed his gun against my neck. 'I've got nothing to lose then,' he said.

'No,' I begged. '*Please*. They know the man at the service station was an accident but if you hurt me now it won't be.'

'You think the truth makes any difference?' Cody sneered. 'Say goodbye to—'

'No.' In a single lunge Flynn reached us. One fist punched at Cody's belly, the other gripped my arm, tugging me away.

A second later I was free. Cody staggered back, still holding the gun.

I turned, took a step to the door.

'Stop!'

I froze. Turned back. Cody's arm was outstretched. His gun waved dangerously in his hand. Flynn pulled me behind him.

'That's enough, Cody,' he demanded.

'Then I'll kill you too,' Cody muttered.

'No.' I couldn't let Flynn put himself in danger like that. My whole body shaking, I stepped sideways, so Flynn and I were now standing next to each other, opposite Cody.

Outside the sound of the car engine had stopped. The whole outside world faded to silence. A thin smile curled around Cody's lips. He steadied his arm and took aim. The gun shook as he pointed it at me.

I stared at Cody's finger on the trigger, my whole life tumbling over inside my head. He was going to shoot. This was it.

A second later, a dark blur flashed in front of me as the shot rang out. Flynn stood suspended for a second between me and Cody, then, like a shadow, he crumpled and fell to the ground. Cody and I stared at each other.

For a split second I thought Cody was going to

shoot me too. Then footsteps sounded on the gravel outside, his face filled with horror and he rushed out of the garage.

I looked down, facing at last what I knew must have happened.

28

Flynn lay on the ground, his eyes shut, blood seeping from his chest.

I dropped to my knees, barely aware of the concrete floor slamming into them, cold and hard. I stared down at Flynn. His eyes flickered open.

'Riv?' he whispered.

'I'm here.' My breath caught in my throat.

Outside, voices were shouting.

A male voice, strong and steady, yelled that he was from the police. Cody shrieked that he had a gun. The first male voice told him to put the gun down.

Barely registering all this, I reached for Flynn's hand.

'It hurts,' he said.

'I know . . .' I looked at his chest. The red was dark, spreading across his shirt. I peeled off my cardigan and pressed it against the wound. 'Wait,

254

I'll get help.' I started to get up, but Flynn held on to my hand.

'Don't go, Riv.' He looked me straight in the eye. 'There isn't time.'

'The police are outside. They can—'

'There isn't time.' Flynn moaned softly. 'I can feel there isn't. *Please*, Riv. I need you to listen.'

I sat forward, my heart in my mouth. I gripped his hand more tightly. 'What? Tell me.'

'Tell Siobhan and Caitlin I love them,' he whispered. 'Tell my mum . . .' He stopped, tears filling his eyes. 'Tell her I'm sorry and I love her too. *So much.*'

A terrible fear swelled inside me. 'You can . . . you can tell them your—'

'No.' Flynn said. 'I can feel it . . . there's not enough time . . . *please.*'

I nodded. Outside on the gravel Cody was still shouting, threatening to shoot someone. I heard Emmi and Grace shrieking with terror. Someone – a man – was yelling at everyone to get back.

I bent closer, my hair brushing over Flynn's face. 'It will be fine,' I murmured, not knowing what I was saying. 'It will all be okay.'

Flynn reached his free hand up to brush the hair off my face. He winced with pain and when he spoke, his voice was so faint I could barely hear it. 'It

255

was always you, Riv,' he whispered. 'It will always be you.'

'I love you so much.' I gulped through the sob that rose inside me.

Flynn closed his eyes.

'No.' My lips trembled. 'You're not leaving me again.'

Flynn's mouth half formed a smile. 'I've never left,' he said softly, his eyes still shut. 'I've been watching over you whenever Bentham left me alone for five minutes.'

'You went back to him . . .'

'Only to protect you, to keep you safe . . .' Flynn's eyes flickered open. 'I was always coming back for you. I could never stay away.'

'I don't want you to stay away. I want you here with me. Forever. Married. Kids. Everything.'

'Me too, more than anything,' Flynn whispered. 'Listen, Riv, there's just one more thing.'

I bent closer. My lips were just over his.

'Live your life,' he breathed. 'Promise me.'

I touched his lips. They were cold. 'I promise.'

I drew back, gazing into his eyes, gold and green and so beautiful. 'You're everything to me,' I whispered. 'Everything.'

Flynn's eyes softened, fixed on me. And then his hand loosened its grip. The world shrank to this moment and the love in his eyes and then the power faded from his face and his expression grew blank and I knew he was gone.

I sat, gazing down at him, unable to believe it.

'Flynn,' I sobbed. I shook his arm. 'Flynn, *please*.'

It couldn't be true.

I pressed my fingers against his neck, felt the inside of his wrist, laid my ear to his chest. There was no pulse. No heartbeat.

The tears dried in my eyes. He was dead.

Outside, Cody was still shouting, still threatening to kill someone.

I looked up, utterly numb.

Outside, a policeman yelled out that this was Cody's final warning. If he didn't put down his gun, the police would shoot.

I stroked Flynn's hair, his face. It wasn't possible. He couldn't no longer exist. Our love was meant to be . . . we were supposed to defy the stars . . . to be together.

Forever.

I looked up. Right in my eyeline, on the shelf above Flynn's head, sat the drill and the screwdrivers and the bits of wood I had noticed earlier. In the middle of the tools a Stanley knife glinted in the light from the door. The blade was short but it looked sharp.

It was a sign.

He was gone. Nothing made sense except that I didn't want to live without him.

I took the knife and held it over my wrist. One slice and blood would flow and I would die.

More shouting outside. A male voice was counting down from five, giving Cody a chance to lay down his gun. I could hear footsteps on the gravel, people being moved back. It was all background noise. Inside my head there was just one voice, one chant, one call for me to take my own life and be with Flynn.

I hesitated, staring down at the Stanley knife. Except I had just promised Flynn to live. Images flashed in front of my eyes: Flynn laughing, Flynn walking towards me, hungry to kiss me, Flynn's eyes burning with anger and longing and love.

More shouts outside but I was no longer listening.

What about my family? There was Stone and Mum and poor Dad. I saw their faces, the misery my death would bring them.

And there was little Lily. The world was hard and she was going to need a big sister.

Flynn's life had been taken from him. I could choose to keep mine.

And I should.

I had a life to live for. And I had promised Flynn I would live it.

My hand trembled as I put the knife back on the shelf.

And then a shot exploded into the night air outside. Emmi screamed out in fear. More shouts and screams. Grace was shrieking.

'What about River?' she was saying. 'Is she okay? What about Leo?'

Why was she asking about Leo?

I wanted to get up and go to the door to see what was happening, but something held me here, where it was just me and Flynn. Just for a few more moments.

'I'm fine.' Leo was speaking now, his voice shaking. He wasn't far away, just outside the door.

I could hear Emmi there too, and James. Their voices were tense and strained. Someone – a policeman, presumably – was stopping them from coming inside the garage.

Another man was speaking into a crackly radio: 'We had to, Cody Walsh wasn't fooling with that gun, sir,' he was saying. 'He would have shot the boy – er, first name, Leo, that's all I know right now. Yes, he would have shot to kill if we hadn't taken him out first.' There was a pause. 'No, sir, we don't know what's happened inside the garage.'

Grace was sobbing. I processed what I'd heard,

feeling strangely numb; so Cody had held Leo hostage and the police had shot him dead.

But Leo and everyone else were okay.

That, at least, was good.

I felt for Flynn's hand again. It was already cold. I stared down at him. All the power of his presence was gone. How was it possible that so much life, so much energy had just been wiped out in a single second.

I lay down beside him on the floor and closed my eyes.

'I'll never love anyone as much as I love you,' I whispered.

Time passed – maybe just a few seconds, maybe longer. Then footsteps sounded across the garage. A light shone right at me, a red glow behind my shut eyes.

'Oh, Jesus.' It was a man's voice.

'River!' That was Leo.

'River!' Grace and Emmi were shouting out my name too.

Their voices rose, calling me to them. '*River!*'

It was time to start living.

I opened my eyes.

Epilogue

Flynn died fifteen years ago and I still think about him every day. I have kept my promise to him to live and have done my best to make it a good life.

Cody's death that terrible night at least meant that I didn't live in fear ever again. It was soon obvious that despite what Flynn had told me about Bentham, there was no way my evidence would be anywhere near enough to prosecute him and after taking a statement, the police never approached me about him again. I still see his name occasionally and he still owns the Blue Parrot but I have never been there again.

I spent the funeral and most of the year after Flynn's death in a daze.

The funeral itself was awful, though, to be honest, it's a blur now. Mostly I remember the sight of the coffin and Dad at my side and the dead look in Flynn's mum's eyes.

James, Grace and Emmi and a lot of our other

friends were there. But Leo wasn't. He had a bit of a breakdown after Cody held him hostage and his dad and Ros took him down to Devon to their new place as soon as they could. I didn't hear from him for a few months but since then we've been in touch on a regular basis. He's fine now – a totally different person from the shy, awkward boy I met all those years ago. He's married – to a really nice girl he met at uni – and I'm godmother to the younger of their two sons.

Dad and Gemma had a second baby too. Daisy was born two years after Lily and, like her, has grown up at the commune. They're teenagers now, and I still see them all the time. I love them both very much, particularly Lily. Sometimes she reminds me of how I was when I met Flynn: wide-eyed and romantic, longing to fall in love and be loved in return.

Flynn's sister Siobhan keeps in touch, though these days it's mostly just texts on birthdays and at Christmas. She's still married to Gary. Together they run a whole network of hair and beauty salons which make them a lot of money. Not that it's changed Siobhan. She's still the same, sweet-natured person even though she and Gary now live in a big house with four kids, three dogs and a hamster. Siobhan and Flynn's mum lives with them too.

Whenever I see her we have a quiet word about Flynn. I think she's the only person who really understands how I feel about him.

Caitlin visits them occasionally, but spends most of her time travelling around Asia and India, living hand to mouth as an artist. I know Siobhan despairs of her, but of all the people I know, Caitlin reminds me most of Flynn. There's the same slightly wild look in her eye. I know their mum worries that she hasn't settled down, but I love to hear about her adventures abroad. It's like she's doing all the things Flynn never had a chance to and I love her for that.

I still see most of my old friends. Emmi lives not far away. She dropped out of uni after just one term to work as a model. It's funny, I would have bet then that it was Emmi who would live the wild life but actually she's settled right down now and is happily married to a banker. I know she really wants kids and though I would never have imagined it when we were younger, I think she'll make a great mum so I hope that happens for her soon. Grace and James stayed together throughout university, then broke up soon after. Compared to me and Flynn, they were pretty chilled about it. There was no big drama, they just both said that the relationship had run its course, that maybe they'd met each other too young for it to last.

I didn't see much of Grace for a while, but we've been close again for a long time now. She's a teacher, living with a really nice guy and their twin boys. We're both still in touch with James, who's a solicitor now and married with a little girl. James is still the same as he always was. He's the only other person, apart from Flynn's mum, who I really talk about Flynn with.

That always makes me sad, even after all this time.

And what have I done with my life? Somehow I got enough A levels to get to uni, where I studied History – just like Flynn had said he wanted to. It was good to get away to somewhere new, where no one knew about my past. I moved back to the commune afterwards and stayed there with Dad and Gemma in Leo's old apartment for a year. There was a new family with a baby in the flat we once lived in and when I went up to take a look at the bedroom Flynn and I had once shared it was unrecognisable – a nursery all painted in pink with ballerina figures on the curtains. I found my old heart bracelet on a chain under the loose floorboard and I still have it, just as I still have the leather string with the little blue 'R' on the end that Flynn kept around his neck.

For a long time it helped me keep him close.

There were many years when I really gave up on other relationships. I tried for a while, dating quite a few guys at uni, but none of them matched up to Flynn. It's funny ... when you're young, adults tell you that your life hasn't really started yet. They say that nothing that has happened so far really counts, that all options are still open, that first love is meaningless.

It isn't true.

I'll never love anyone with the same intensity that I loved Flynn. Maybe that's a good thing. Maybe Flynn and I would have burned out eventually. Maybe it's all happened just as it was supposed to.

One thing I know for sure is that loving Flynn and living with his death brought me closer to Mum and Stone than I probably would ever have been otherwise. You see, like Dad and Gemma and my sisters they love me. And now I know that when people love you, you make it count.

My family and friends helped me through. So did writing. That's what I do now: write stories. I've written lots of books but these are the only ones that tell the truth about who I am.

But it's my son who really turned things around for me. He was conceived by accident and born, a week earlier than expected, on the tenth anniversary of Flynn's death. I knew that night, that his birth was a sign that Flynn had been right to make me live and I had been right to promise I would.

From then on, I opened up, letting myself love and be loved. I made a proper commitment to my son's father, Will, and a few months later we got married.

Will is a good man, a lot easier than Flynn ever was, that's for sure. And I love him. Not with the same blazing passion that Flynn and I loved each other but with something calmer and steadier, that brings me a level of contentment I used to think would never be possible.

Even so, there are still nights when I dream of Flynn and how he sacrificed his own life to save mine. And there's a part of me that will always be his, that still lives inside our love for each other even after all these years

I don't regret a second of our time together. Because Flynn was right that our love was meant to be . . . every bit of it, from tip to tail.

In our heads. In our hearts.

And in the stars.

Forever.